PENGUIN P...

ROMANTIC POETRY

SELECTED BY
PAUL DRIVER

PENGUIN BOOKS
A PENGUIN/GODFREY CAVE EDITION

PENGUIN BOOKS

Published by the Penguin Group
Penguin Books Ltd, 27 Wrights Lane, London w8 5tz, England
Penguin Books USA Inc., 375 Hudson Street, New York, New York 10014, USA
Penguin Books Australia Ltd, Ringwood, Victoria, Australia
Penguin Books Canada Ltd, 10 Alcorn Avenue, Toronto, Ontario, Canada m4v 3b2
Penguin Books (NZ) Ltd, 182–190 Wairau Road, Auckland 10, New Zealand

Penguin Books Ltd, Registered Offices: Harmondsworth, Middlesex, England

This edition first published 1995
Published in Penguin Popular Classics 1996
1 3 5 7 9 10 8 6 4 2

Selection copyright © Paul Driver, 1995

Set in 9/11 pt Ehrhardt Monotype
Typeset by Datix International Limited, Bungay, Suffolk
Printed in England by Clays Ltd, St Ives plc

ISBN 0 14 062202 0

CONTENTS

The Tyger, WILLIAM BLAKE   1
The Smile, WILLIAM BLAKE   1
Nurse's Song, WILLIAM BLAKE   2
Nurse's Song, WILLIAM BLAKE   3
The Everlasting Gospel, WILLIAM BLAKE   3
The School Boy, WILLIAM BLAKE   3
The Fly, WILLIAM BLAKE   4
'Jerusalem', WILLIAM BLAKE   5
John Barleycorn: A Ballad, ROBERT BURNS   6
Auguries of Innocence, WILLIAM BLAKE   8
The Chimney Sweeper, WILLIAM BLAKE   11
The Chimney Sweeper, WILLIAM BLAKE   12
The Garden of Love, WILLIAM BLAKE   12
The Clod and the Pebble, WILLIAM BLAKE   13
London, WILLIAM BLAKE   13
The Human Abstract, WILLIAM BLAKE   14
To a Mouse, ROBERT BURNS   15
My Bony Mary, ROBERT BURNS   16
Frost at Midnight, SAMUEL TAYLOR COLERIDGE   17
The Lamb, WILLIAM BLAKE   19
Infant Sorrow, WILLIAM BLAKE   20
The Knight's Tomb, SAMUEL TAYLOR COLERIDGE   20
The Divine Image, WILLIAM BLAKE   20
The Sick Rose, WILLIAM BLAKE   21
Duty Surviving Self-love, SAMUEL TAYLOR COLERIDGE   21
To the Evening Star, WILLIAM BLAKE   22
'My heart leaps up when I behold',
    WILLIAM WORDSWORTH   22
To Winter, WILLIAM BLAKE   23
The Cataract of Lodore, ROBERT SOUTHEY   23
A Red, Red Rose, ROBERT BURNS   27
Ae Fond Kiss, ROBERT BURNS   27
'O whistle, and I'll come to ye, my lad', ROBERT BURNS   28

The Banks o' Doon, ROBERT BURNS 29

The Solitary Reaper, WILLIAM WORDSWORTH 29

For a' that and a' that, ROBERT BURNS 30

Dejection: An Ode, SAMUEL TAYLOR COLERIDGE 32

Ah! Sun-flower, WILLIAM BLAKE 36

To a Butterfly, WILLIAM WORDSWORTH 36

'Strange fits of passion have I known',
  WILLIAM WORDSWORTH 37

'She walks in beauty', LORD BYRON 38

Stanzas for Music, LORD BYRON 38

'She dwelt among the untrodden ways',
  WILLIAM WORDSWORTH 39

'A slumber did my spirit seal', WILLIAM WORDSWORTH 39

Ozymandias, PERCY BYSSHE SHELLEY 40

Ode to the West Wind, PERCY BYSSHE SHELLEY 40

Kubla Khan, SAMUEL TAYLOR COLERIDGE 43

An Answer to the Parson, ANON. 44

Sonnet: England in 1819, PERCY BYSSHE SHELLEY 44

The Destruction of Sennacherib, LORD BYRON 45

Lines, PERCY BYSSHE SHELLEY 46

'Remember thee! remember thee!', LORD BYRON 47

Hellas, PERCY BYSSHE SHELLEY 47

'When we two parted', LORD BYRON 48

To a Skylark, PERCY BYSSHE SHELLEY 49

Stanzas: Written in Dejection, near Naples,
  PERCY BYSSHE SHELLEY 52

from The Mask of Anarchy, PERCY BYSSHE SHELLEY 54

'There was a boy', WILLIAM WORDSWORTH 56

To a Skylark, WILLIAM WORDSWORTH 57

The Netherlands, SAMUEL TAYLOR COLERIDGE 57

'Great things are done', ANON. 58

The Cloud, PERCY BYSSHE SHELLEY 58

'The spell is broke, the charm is flown', LORD BYRON 60

La Belle Dame sans Merci: A Ballad, JOHN KEATS 61

'So we'll go no more a-roving', LORD BYRON 62

Song, PERCY BYSSHE SHELLEY 63

Ode to a Nightingale, JOHN KEATS 63

Verse, WALTER SAVAGE LANDOR 65

Cologne, SAMUEL TAYLOR COLERIDGE   66

Song to the Men of England, PERCY BYSSHE SHELLEY   66

Lines Composed a Few Miles above Tintern Abbey . . .

   WILLIAM WORDSWORTH   67

'Bright star! would I were steadfast as thou art',

   JOHN KEATS   71

To Autumn, JOHN KEATS   72

Rondeau, JAMES LEIGH HUNT   73

A Sonnet, PERCY BYSSHE SHELLEY   73

Hesperus, JOHN CLARE   74

Ode on a Grecian Urn, JOHN KEATS   74

'This living hand, now warm and capable', JOHN KEATS   76

'I am', JOHN CLARE   76

'After dark vapours have oppressed our plains',

   JOHN KEATS   77

To Sleep, JOHN KEATS   77

The Yellowhammer, JOHN CLARE   78

Winter Evening, JOHN CLARE   78

First Sight of Spring, JOHN CLARE   79

Snow Storm, JOHN CLARE   79

Night Wind, JOHN CLARE   80

Evening Schoolboys, JOHN CLARE   80

Composed Upon Westminster Bridge, September 3, 1802,

   WILLIAM WORDSWORTH   81

'I wandered lonely as a cloud', WILLIAM WORDSWORTH   81

The Badger, JOHN CLARE   82

On the Grasshopper and Cricket, JOHN KEATS   84

'Over the hill and over the dale', JOHN KEATS   85

'Old Meg she was a gipsy', JOHN KEATS   85

Nutting, WILLIAM WORDSWORTH   86

Autumn, JOHN CLARE   88

Haymaking, JOHN CLARE   88

Old Man Travelling, WILLIAM WORDSWORTH   89

London, 1802, WILLIAM WORDSWORTH   90

Autumn Morning, JOHN CLARE   90

The Small Celandine, WILLIAM WORDSWORTH   91

Evening, JOHN CLARE   91

The Mermaidens' Vesper-hymn, GEORGE DARLEY   92

Eternity, WILLIAM BLAKE   93
'Surprised by joy', WILLIAM WORDSWORTH   93
The Rime of the Ancient Mariner, SAMUEL TAYLOR
   COLERIDGE   93

The Tyger

Tyger, Tyger, burning bright,
In the forests of the night:
What immortal hand or eye,
Could frame thy fearful symmetry?

In what distant deeps or skies
Burnt the fire of thine eyes!
On what wings dare he aspire?
What the hand, dare sieze the fire?

And what shoulder, & what art,
Could twist the sinews of thy heart?
And when thy heart began to beat,
What dread hand? & what dread feet?

What the hammer? what the chain,
In what furnace was thy brain?
What the anvil? what dread grasp,
Dare its deadly terrors clasp?

When the stars threw down their spears
And water'd heaven with their tears:
Did he smile his work to see?
Did he who made the Lamb make thee?

Tyger, Tyger, burning bright,
In the forests of the night:
What immortal hand or eye,
Dare frame thy fearful symmetry?

WILLIAM BLAKE

The Smile

There is a Smile of Love
And there is a Smile of Deceit
And there is a Smile of Smiles
In which these two Smiles meet.

I

And there is a Frown of Hate
And there is a Frown of disdain
And there is a Frown of Frowns
Which you strive to forget in vain

For it sticks in the Heart's deep Core
And it sticks in the deep Back bone
And no Smile that ever was smil'd
But only one Smile alone.

That betwixt the Cradle & Grave
It only once Smil'd can be,
But when it once is Smil'd
There's an end to all Misery.

WILLIAM BLAKE

Nurse's Song

When the voices of children are heard on the green
And laughing is heard on the hill,
My heart is at rest within my breast
And every thing else is still.

Then come home my children, the sun is gone down
And the dews of night arise
Come come leave off play, and let us away
Till the morning appears in the skies.

No no let us play, for it is yet day
And we cannot go to sleep
Besides in the sky, the little birds fly
And the hills are all covered with sheep.

Well well go & play till the light fades away
And then go home to bed
The little ones leaped & shouted & laugh'd
And all the hills ecchoed.

WILLIAM BLAKE

Nurse's Song

When the voices of children are heard on the green
And whisperings are in the dale:
The days of my youth rise fresh in my mind,
My face turns green and pale.

Then come home my children, the sun is gone down
And the dews of night arise
Your spring & your day, are wasted in play
And your winter and night in disguise.

WILLIAM BLAKE

The Everlasting Gospel

To the Accuser who is
the God of this World

Truly, my Satan, thou art but a dunce
And dost not know the garment from the man:
Every harlot was a virgin once,
Nor canst thou ever change Kate into Nan.

Though thou art worshipped by the names divine
Of Jesus and Jehovah, thou art still
The Son of Morn in weary night's decline,
The lost traveller's dream under the hill.

WILLIAM BLAKE

The School Boy

I love to rise in a summer morn,
When the birds sing on every tree;
The distant huntsman winds his horn,
And the sky-lark sings with me.
O! what sweet company.

3

But to go to school in a summer morn
O! it drives all joy away;
Under a cruel eye outworn,
The little ones spend the day,
In sighing and dismay.

Ah! then at times I drooping sit,
And spend many an anxious hour.
Nor in my book can I take delight,
Nor sit in learnings bower,
Worn thro' with the dreary shower

How can the bird that is born for joy,
Sit in a cage and sing.
How can a child when fears annoy,
But droop his tender wing,
And forget his youthful spring.

O! father & mother, if buds are nip'd,
And blossoms blown away,
And if the tender plants arc strip'd
Of their joy in the springing day,
By sorrow and cares dismay,

How shall the summer arise in joy
Or the summer fruits appear
Or how shall we gather what griefs destroy
Or bless the mellowing year,
When the blasts of winter appear.

WILLIAM BLAKE

The Fly

Little Fly
Thy summers play,
My thoughtless hand
Has brush'd away.

Am not I
A fly like thee?

Or art not thou
A man like me?

For I dance
And drink & sing;
Till some blind hand
Shall brush my wing.

If thought is life
And strength & breath;
And the want
Of thought is death;

Then am I
A happy fly,
If I live,
Or if I die.

WILLIAM BLAKE

'Jerusalem'

And did those feet in ancient time
Walk upon England's mountains green?
And was the holy Lamb of God
On England's pleasant pastures seen?

And did the Countenance Divine
Shine forth upon our clouded hills?
And was Jerusalem builded here
Among these dark Satanic mills?

Bring me my bow of burning gold;
Bring me my arrows of desire;
Bring me my spear – O clouds, unfold!
Bring me my chariot of fire!

I will not cease from mental fight,
Nor shall my sword sleep in my hand,
Till we have built Jerusalem,
In England's green and pleasant land.

WILLIAM BLAKE

John Barleycorn: A Ballad

There was three kings into the east,
  Three kings both great and high,
And they hae sworn a solemn oath
  John Barleycorn should die.

They took a plough and plough'd him down,
  Put clods upon his head,
And they hae sworn a solemn oath
  John Barleycorn was dead.

But the chearful Spring came kindly on,
  And show'rs began to fall;
John Barleycorn got up again,
  And sore surpris'd them all.

The sultry suns of Summer came,
  And he grew thick and strong,
His head weel arm'd wi' pointed spears,
  That no one should him wrong.

The sober Autumn enter'd mild,
  When he grew wan and pale;
His bending joints and drooping head
  Show'd he began to fail.

His colour sicken'd more and more,
  He faded into age;
And then his enemies began
  To show their deadly rage.

They've taen a weapon, long and sharp,
  And cut him by the knee;
Then ty'd him fast upon a cart,
  Like a rogue for forgerie.

They laid him down upon his back,
  And cudgell'd him full sore;
They hung him up before the storm,
  And turn'd him o'er and o'er.

They filled up a darksome pit
    With water to the brim,
They heaved in John Barleycorn,
    There let him sink or swim.

They laid him out upon the floor,
    To work him farther woe,
And still, as signs of life appear'd,
    They toss'd him to and fro.

They wasted, o'er a scorching flame,
    The marrow of his bones;
But a Miller us'd him worst of all,
    For he crush'd him between two stones.

And they hae taen his very heart's blood,
    And drank it round and round;
And still the more and more they drank,
    Their joy did more abound.

John Barleycorn was a hero bold,
    Of noble enterprise,
For if you do but taste his blood,
    'Twill make your courage rise.

'Twill make a man forget his woe;
    'Twill heighten all his joy:
'Twill make the widow's heart to sing,
    Tho' the tear were in her eye.

Then let us toast John Barleycorn,
    Each man a glass in hand;
And may his great posterity
    Ne'er fail in old Scotland!

ROBERT BURNS

To see a World in a Grain of Sand
And a Heaven in a Wild Flower
Hold Infinity in the palm of your hand
And Eternity in an hour.
A Robin Red breast in a Cage
Puts all Heaven in a Rage.
A dove house fill'd with doves & Pigeons
Shudders Hell thro all its regions.
A dog starv'd at his Master's Gate
Predicts the ruin of the State.
A Horse misus'd upon the Road
Calls to Heaven for Human blood.
Each outcry of the hunted Hare
A fibre from the Brain does tear.
A Skylark wounded in the wing,
A Cherubim does cease to sing.
The Game Cock clip'd & arm'd for fight
Does the Rising Sun affright.
Every Wolf's & Lion's howl
Raises from Hell a Human Soul.
The wild deer wand'ring here & there
Keeps the Human Soul from Care.
The Lamb misus'd breeds Public strife
And yet forgives the Butcher's Knife.
The Bat that flits at close of Eve
Has left the Brain that won't Believe.
The Owl that calls upon the Night
Speaks the Unbeliever's fright.
He who shall hurt the little Wren.
Shall never be belov'd by Men.
He who the Ox to wrath has mov'd
Shall never be by Woman lov'd.
The wanton Boy that kills the Fly
Shall feel the Spider's enmity.
He who torments the Chafer's sprite
Weaves a Bower in endless Night.

The Catterpiller on the Leaf
Repeats to thee thy Mother's grief.
Kill not the Moth nor Butterfly,
For the Last Judgment draweth nigh.
He who shall train the Horse to War
Shall never pass the Polar Bar.
The Begger's Dog & Widow's Cat,
Feed them & thou wilt grow fat.
The Gnat that sings his Summer's song
Poison gets from Slander's tongue.
The poison of the Snake & Newt
Is the sweat of Envy's Foot.
The Poison of the Honey Bee
Is the Artist's Jealousy.
The Prince's Robes & Beggar's Rags
Are Toadstools on the Miser's Bags.
A truth that's told with bad intent
Beats all the Lies you can invent.
It is right it should be so:
Man was made for Joy & Woe;
And when this we rightly know
Thro' the World we safely go.
Joy & Woe are woven fine,
A Clothing for the Soul divine;
Under every grief & pine
Runs a joy with silken twine.
The Babe is more than swadling Bands;
Throughout all these Human Lands
Tools were made & Born were hands,
Every Farmer Understands.
Every Tear from Every Eye
Becomes a Babe in Eternity;
This is caught by Females bright
And return'd to its own delight.
The Bleat, the Bark, Bellow & Roar
Are Waves that Beat on Heaven's Shore.
The Babe that weeps the Rod beneath
Writes Revenge in realms of death.
The Beggar's Rags, fluttering in Air,

Does to Rags the Heavens tear.
The Soldier arm'd with Sword & Gun,
Palsied, strikes the Summer's Sun.
The poor Man's Farthing is worth more
Than all the Gold on Africs Shore.
One Mite wrung from the Lab'rer's hands
Shall buy & sell the Miser's Lands;
Or if protected from on high,
Does that whole Nation sell & buy.
He who mocks the Infant's Faith
Shall be mock'd in Age & Death.
He who shall teach the Child to Doubt
The rotting Grave shall ne'er get out.
He who respects the Infant's faith
Triumphs over Hell & Death.
The Child's Toys & the Old Man's Reasons
Are the Fruits of the Two seasons.
The Questioner, who sits so sly,
Shall never know how to Reply.
He who replies to words of Doubt
Doth put the Light of Knowledge out.
The Strongest Poison ever known
Came from Caesar's Laurel Crown.
Nought can deform the Human Race
Like to the Armour's iron brace.
When Gold & Gems adorn the Plow
To peaceful Arts shall Envy Bow.
A Riddle or the Cricket's Cry
Is to Doubt a fit Reply.
The Emmet's Inch & Eagle's Mile
Make Lame Philosophy to smile.
He who Doubts from what he sees
Will ne'er Believe, do what you Please.
If the Sun & Moon should doubt,
They'd immediately Go out.
To be in a Passion you Good may do,
But no Good if a Passion is in you.
The Whore & Gambler, by the State
Licenc'd, build that Nation's Fate.

The Harlot's cry from Street to Street
Shall weave Old England's winding Sheet.
The Winner's Shout, the Loser's Curse,
Dance before dead England's Hearse.
Every Night & every Morn
Some to Misery are Born.
Every Morn & every Night
Some are Born to sweet delight.
Some are Born to sweet delight,
Some are Born to Endless Night.
We are led to Believe a Lie
When we see [*with*] not Thro the Eye
Which was Born in a Night to perish in a Night
When the Soul Slept in Beams of Light.
God Appears & God is Light
To those poor Souls who dwell in Night,
But does a Human Form Display
To those who Dwell in Realms of day.

WILLIAM BLAKE

The Chimney Sweeper

When my mother died I was very young,
And my father sold me while yet my tongue,
Could scarcely cry weep weep weep weep.
So your chimneys I sweep & in soot I sleep.

There's little Tom Dacre, who cried when his head
That curl'd like a lambs back, was shav'd, so I said.
Hush Tom never mind it, for when your head's bare,
You know that the soot cannot spoil your white hair.

And so he was quiet, & that very night,
As Tom was a sleeping he had such a slight,
That thousands of sweepers Dick, Joe Ned & Jack
Were all of them lock'd up in coffins of black

And by came an Angel who had a bright key,
And he open'd the coffins & set them all free.

Then down a green plain leaping laughing they run
And wash in a river and shine in the Sun.

Then naked & white, all their bags left behind,
They rise upon clouds, and sport in the wind.
And the Angel told Tom if he'd be a good boy,
He'd have God for his father & never want joy.

And so Tom awoke and we rose in the dark
And got with our bags & our brushes to work.
Tho' the morning was cold, Tom was happy & warm,
So if all do their duty, they need not fear harm.

WILLIAM BLAKE

The Chimney Sweeper

A little black thing among the snow:
Crying 'weep! weep!' in notes of woe!
Where are thy father & mother? say?
They are both gone up to the church to pray.

Because I was happy upon the heath.
And smil'd among the winters snow:
They clothed me in the clothes of death.
And taught me to sing the notes of woe.

And because I am happy & dance & sing.
They think they have done me no injury:
And are gone to praise God & his Priest & King
Who make up a heaven of our misery.

WILLIAM BLAKE

The Garden of Love

I went to the Garden of Love.
And saw what I never had seen:
A Chapel was built in the midst,
Where I used to play on the green.

And the gates of this Chapel were shut,
And Thou shalt not. writ over the door;
So I turn'd to the Garden of Love,
That so many sweet flowers bore.

And I saw it was filled with graves,
And tomb-stones where flowers should be:
And priests in black gowns, were walking their rounds,
And binding with briars, my joys & desires.

WILLIAM BLAKE

The Clod and the Pebble

Love seeketh not Itself to please,
Nor for itself hath any care;
But for another gives its ease,
And builds a Heaven in Hells despair.

So sang a little Clod of Clay,
Trodden with the cattles feet:
But a Pebble of the brook,
Warbled out these metres meet.

Love seeketh only Self to please,
To bind another to its delight;
Joys in anothers loss of ease,
And builds a Hell in Heavens despite.

WILLIAM BLAKE

London

I wander thro' each charter'd street,
Near where the charter'd Thames does flow.
And mark in every face I meet
Marks of weakness, marks of woe.

In every cry of every Man,
In every Infants cry of fear,
In every voice: in every ban,
The mind-forg'd manacles I hear

How the Chimney-sweeper's cry
Every black'ning Church appalls,
And the hapless Soldier's sigh,
Runs in blood down Palace walls.

But most thro' midnight streets I hear
How the youthful Harlots curse
Blasts the new-born Infants tear,
And blights with plagues the Marriage hearse.

WILLIAM BLAKE

The Human Abstract

Pity would be no more,
If we did not make somebody Poor:
And Mercy no more could be,
If all were as happy as we;

And mutual fear brings peace;
Till the selfish loves increase.
Then Cruelty knits a snare,
And spreads his baits with care.

He sits down with holy fears,
And waters the ground with tears:
Then Humility takes its root
Underneath his foot.

Soon spreads the dismal shade
Of Mystery over his head;
And the Catterpiller and Fly,
Feed on the Mystery.

And it bears the fruit of Deceit,
Ruddy and sweet to eat;
And the Raven his nest has made
In its thickest shade.

The Gods of the earth and sea,
Sought thro' Nature to find this Tree
But their search was all in vain:
There grows one in the Human Brain.

WILLIAM BLAKE

To a Mouse

ON TURNING HER UP IN HER NEST WITH THE PLOUGH,
NOVEMBER 1785

Wee, sleeket, cowran, tim'rous *beastie*,
O, what a panic's in thy breastie!
Thou need na start awa sae hasty,
　　　　Wi' bickering brattle!
I wad be laith to rin an' chase thee,
　　　　Wi' murd'ring *pattle*!

I'm truly sorry Man's dominion
Has broken Nature's social union,
An' justifies that ill opinion,
　　　　Which makes thee startle,
At me, thy poor, earth-born companion,
　　　　An' *fellow-mortal*!

I doubt na, whyles, but thou may thieve;
What then? poor beastie, thou maun live!
A *daimen-icker* in a *thrave*
　　　　'S a sma' request:
I'll get a blessin wi' the lave,
　　　　An' never miss't!

Thy wee-bit *housie*, too, in ruin!
It's silly wa's the win's are strewin!
An' naething, now, to big a new ane,
　　　　O' foggage green!
An' bleak December's winds ensuin,
　　　　Baith snell an' keen!

Thou saw the fields laid bare an' wast,
An' weary Winter comin fast,
An' cozie here, beneath the blast,
                    Thou thought to dwell,
Till crash! the cruel *coulter* past
                    Out thro' thy cell.

That wee-bit heap o' leaves an' stibble,
Has cost thee monie a weary nibble!
Now thou's turn'd out, for a' thy trouble,
                    But house or hald,
To thole the Winter's sleety dribble,
                    An' *cranreuch* cauld!

But Mousie, thou art no thy-lane,
In proving *foresight* may be vain:
The best laid schemes o' *Mice* an' *Men*,
                    Gang aft agley,
An' lea'e us nought but grief an' pain,
                    For promis'd joy!

Still, thou art blest, compar'd wi' *me*!
The *present* only toucheth thee:
But Och! I *backward* cast my e'e,
                    On prospects drear!
An' *forward*, tho' I canna *see*,
                    I *guess* an' *fear*!

ROBERT BURNS

My Bony Mary

Go fetch to me a pint o' wine,
    And fill it in a silver tassie;
That I may drink, before I go,
    A service to my bonie lassie:
The boat rocks at the Pier o' Leith,
    Fu' loud the wind blaws frae the Ferry,
The ship rides by the Berwick-law,
    And I maun leave my bony Mary.

The trumpets sound, the banners fly,
    The glittering spears are ranked ready,
The shouts o' war are heard afar,
    The battle closes deep and bloody.
It's not the roar o' sea or shore,
    Wad make me langer wish to tarry;
Nor shouts o' war that's heard afar –
    It's leaving thee, my bony Mary!

ROBERT BURNS

Frost at Midnight

The Frost performs its secret ministry,
Unhelped by any wind. The owlet's cry
Came loud – and hark, again! loud as before.
The inmates of my cottage, all at rest,
Have left me to that solitude, which suits
Abstruser musings: save that at my side
My cradled infant slumbers peacefully.
'Tis calm indeed! so calm, that it disturbs
And vexes meditation with its strange
And extreme silentness. Sea, hill, and wood,
This populous village! Sea, and hill, and wood,
With all the numberless goings-on of life,
Inaudible as dreams! the thin blue flame
Lies on my low-burnt fire, and quivers not;
Only that film, which fluttered on the grate,
Still flutters there, the sole unquiet thing.
Methinks, its motion in this hush of nature
Gives it dim sympathies with me who live,
Making it a companionable form,
Whose puny flaps and freaks the idling Spirit
By its own moods interprets, every where
Echo or mirror seeking of itself,
And makes a toy of Thought.
                                But O! how oft,
How oft, at school, with most believing mind,
Presageful, have I gazed upon the bars,
To watch that fluttering *stranger*! and as oft

With unclosed lids, already had I dreamt
Of my sweet birth-place, and the old church-tower,
Whose bells, the poor man's only music, rang
From morn to evening, all the hot Fair-day,
So sweetly, that they stirred and haunted me
With a wild pleasure, falling on mine ear .
Most like articulate sounds of things to come!
So gazed I, till the soothing things, I dreamt,
Lulled me to sleep, and sleep prolonged my dreams!
And so I brooded all the following morn,
Awed by the stern preceptor's face, mine eye
Fixed with mock study on my swimming book:
Save if the door half opened, and I snatched
A hasty glance, and still my heart leaped up,
For still I hoped to see the *stranger's* face,
Townsman, or aunt, or sister more beloved,
My play-mate when we both were clothed alike!

   Dear Babe, that sleepest cradled by my side,
Whose gentle breathings, heard in this deep calm,
Fill up the interspersèd vacancies
And momentary pauses of the thought!
My babe so beautiful! it thrills my heart
With tender gladness, thus to look at thee,
And think that thou shalt learn far other lore,
And in far other scenes! For I was reared
In the great city, pent 'mid cloisters dim,
And saw nought lovely but the sky and stars.
But *thou*, my babe! shalt wander like a breeze
By lakes and sandy shores, beneath the crags
Of ancient mountain, and beneath the clouds,
Which image in their bulk both lakes and shores
And mountain crags: so shalt thou see and hear
The lovely shapes and sounds intelligible
Of that eternal language, which thy God
Utters, who from eternity doth teach
Himself in all, and all things in himself.
Great universal Teacher! he shall mould
Thy spirit, and by giving make it ask.

Therefore all seasons shall be sweet to thee,
Whether the summer clothe the general earth
With greenness, or the redbreast sit and sing
Betwixt the tufts of snow on the bare branch
Of mossy apple-tree, while the nigh thatch
Smokes in the sun-thaw; whether the eave-drops fall
Heard only in the trances of the blast,
Or if the secret ministry of frost
Shall hang them up in silent icicles,
Quietly shining to the quiet Moon.

SAMUEL TAYLOR COLERIDGE

The Lamb

Little Lamb who made thee
Dost thou know who made thee
Gave thee life & bid thee feed?
By the stream & o'er the mead;
Gave thee clothing of delight,
Softest clothing wooly bright;
Gave thee such a tender voice,
Making all the vales rejoice:
Little Lamb who made thee
Dost thou know who made thee?

Little Lamb I'll tell thee,
Little Lamb I'll tell thee:
He is called by thy name,
For he calls himself a Lamb:
He is meek & he is mild,
He became a little child:
I a child & thou a lamb,

We are called by his name.
Little Lamb God bless thee.
Little Lamb God bless thee.

WILLIAM BLAKE

Infant Sorrow

My mother groand! my father wept.
Into the dangerous world I leapt:
Helpless, naked, piping loud;
Like a fiend hid in a cloud.

Struggling in my fathers hands:
Striving against my swadling bands:
Bound and weary I thought best
To sulk upon my mother's breast.

WILLIAM BLAKE

The Knight's Tomb

Where is the grave of Sir Arthur O'Kellyn?
Where may the grave of that good man be? –
By the side of a spring, on the breast of Helvellyn,
Under the twigs of a young birch tree!
The oak that in summer was sweet to hear,
And rustled its leaves in the fall of the year,
And whistled and roared in the winter alone,
Is gone, – and the birch in its stead is grown. –
The Knight's bones are dust
And his good sword rust; –
His soul is with the saints, I trust.

SAMUEL TAYLOR COLERIDGE

The Divine Image

To Mercy, Pity, Peace, and Love,
All pray in their distress;
And to these virtues of delight
Return their thankfulness.

For Mercy, Pity, Peace, and Love,
Is God, our father dear:

And Mercy, Pity, Peace, and Love,
Is Man, his child and care.

For Mercy has a human heart,
Pity, a human face,
And Love, the human form divine,
And Peace, the human dress.

Then every man of every clime,
That prays in his distress,
Prays to the human form divine
Love, Mercy, Pity, Peace.

And all must love the human form,
In heathen, turk or jew.
Where Mercy, Love & Pity dwell
There God is dwelling too.

WILLIAM BLAKE

The Sick Rose

O Rose, thou art sick.
The invisible worm,
That flies in the night
In the howling storm:

Has found out thy bed
Of crimson joy:
And his dark secret love
Does thy life destroy.

WILLIAM BLAKE

Duty Surviving Self-love

THE ONLY SURE FRIEND OF DECLINING LIFE

A SOLILOQUY

Unchanged within, to see all changed without,
Is a blank lot and hard to bear, no doubt.

Yet why at others' wanings should'st thou fret?
Then only might'st thou feel a just regret,
Hadst thou withheld thy love or hid thy light
In selfish forethought of neglect and slight.
O wiselier then, from feeble yearnings freed,
While, and on whom, thou may'st – shine on! nor heed
Whether the object by reflected light
Return thy radiance or absorb it quite:
And though thou notest from thy safe recess
Old Friends burn dim, like lamps in noisome air,
Love them for what they are; nor love them less,
Because to thee they are not what they were.

SAMUEL TAYLOR COLERIDGE

To the Evening Star

Thou fair-hair'd angel of the evening,
Now, while the sun rests on the mountains, light
Thy bright torch of love; thy radiant crown
Put on, and smile upon our evening bed!
Smile on our loves; and, while thou drawest the
Blue curtains of the sky, scatter thy silver dew
On every flower that shuts its sweet eyes
In timely sleep. Let thy west wind sleep on
The lake; speak of si[l]ence with thy glimmering eyes,
And wash the dusk with silver. Soon, full soon,
Dost thou withdraw; then the wolf rages wide,
And the lion glares thro' the dun forest:
The fleeces of our flocks are cover'd with
Thy sacred dew: protect them with thine influence.

WILLIAM BLAKE

'My heart leaps up when I behold'

My heart leaps up when I behold
    A rainbow in the sky:
So was it when my life began;
So is it now I am a man;

So be it when I shall grow old,
   Or let me die!
The Child is father of the Man;
And I could wish my days to be
Bound each to each by natural piety.

WILLIAM WORDSWORTH

To Winter

O Winter! bar thine adamantine doors:
The north is thine; there has thou built thy dark
Deep-founded habitation. Shake not thy roofs,
Nor bend thy pillars with thine iron car.

He hears me not, but o'er the yawning deep
Rides heavy; his storms are unchain'd; sheathed
In ribbed steel, I dare not lift mine eyes;
For he hath rear'd his sceptre o'er the world.

Lo! now the direful monster, whose skin clings
To his strong bones, strides o'er the groaning rocks:
He withers all in silence, and his hand
Unclothes the earth, and freezes up frail life.

He takes his seat upon the cliffs, the mariner
Cries in vain. Poor little wretch! that deal'st
With storms; till heaven smiles, and the monster
Is driv'n yelling to his caves beneath mount Hecla.

WILLIAM BLAKE

The Cataract of Lodore

DESCRIBED IN RHYMES FOR THE NURSERY

'How does the Water
Come down at Lodore?'
My little boy ask'd me
Thus, once on a time;
And moreover he task'd me

23

To tell him in rhyme.
Anon at the word,
There first came one daughter
And then came another,
To second and third
The request of their brother,
And to hear how the water
Comes down at Lodore,
With its rush and its roar,
As many a time
They had seen it before.
So I told them in rhyme,
For of rhymes I had store:
And 'twas in my vocation
For their recreation
That so I should sing;
Because I was Laureate
To them and the King.

From its sources which well
In the Tarn on the fell;
From its fountains
In the mountains,
Its rills and its gills;
Through moss and through brake,
It runs and it creeps
For awhile, till it sleeps
In its own little Lake.
And thence at departing,
Awakening and starting,
It runs through the reeds
And away it proceeds,
Through meadow and glade,
In sun and in shade,
And through the wood-shelter,
Among crags in its flurry,
Helter-skelter,
Hurry-scurry.
Here it comes sparkling,

And there it lies darkling;
Now smoaking and frothing
Its tumult and wrath in,
Till in this rapid race
On which it is bent,
It reaches the place
Of its steep descent.

The Cataract strong
Then plunges along,
Striking and raging
As if a war waging
Its caverns and rocks among:
Rising and leaping,
Sinking and creeping,
Swelling and sweeping,
Showering and springing,
Flying and flinging,
Writhing and ringing,
Eddying and whisking,
Spouting and frisking,
Turning and twisting,
Around and around
With endless rebound!
Smiting and fighting,
A sight to delight in;
Confounding, astounding,
Dizzing and deafening the ear with its
sound.

Collecting, projecting,
Receding and speeding,
And shocking and rocking,
And darting and parting,
And threading and spreading,
And whizzing and hissing,
And dripping and skipping,
And hitting and splitting,
And shining and twining,

And rattling and battling,
And shaking and quaking,
And pouring and roaring,
And waving and raving,
And tossing and crossing,
And flowing and going,
And running and stunning,
And foaming and roaming,
And dinning and spinning,
And dropping and hopping,
And working and jerking,
And guggling and struggling,
And heaving and cleaving,
And moaning and groaning;

And glittering and frittering,
And gathering and feathering,
And whitening and brightening,
And quivering and shivering,
And hurrying and skurrying,
And thundering and floundering;

Dividing and gliding and sliding,
And falling and brawling and sprawling,
And driving and riving and striving,
And sprinkling and twinkling and wrinkling,
And sounding and bounding and rounding,
And bubbling and troubling and doubling,
And grumbling rumbling and tumbling,
And clattering battering and shattering;

Retreating and beating and meeting and sheeting,
Delaying and straying and playing and spraying,
Advancing and prancing and glancing and dancing,
Recoiling, turmoiling and toiling and boiling,
And gleaming and streaming and steam ing and beaming,
And rushing and flushing and brushing and gushing,
And flapping and rapping and clapping and slapping,
And curling and whirling and purling and twirling,
And thumping and plumping and bump ing and jumping,

And dashing and flashing and splashing and clashing;
And so never ending, but always descending,
Sounds and motions for ever and ever are blending,
All at once and all o'er, with a mighty uproar,
And this way the Water comes down at Lodore.

ROBERT SOUTHEY

A Red, Red Rose

My luve is like a red, red rose,
  That's newly sprung in June:
My luve is like the melodie,
  That's sweetly play'd in tune.
As fair art thou, my bonie lass,
  So deep in luve am I,
And I will luve thee still, my dear,
  Till a' the seas gang dry.

Till a' the seas gang dry, my dear,
  And the rocks melt wi' the sun!
And I will luve thee still, my dear,
  While the sands o' life shall run.
And fare-thee-weel, my only luve,
  And fare-thee-weel, a while!
And I will come again, my luve,
  Tho' it were ten-thousand mile.

ROBERT BURNS

Ae Fond Kiss

Ae fond kiss and then we sever;
Ae fareweel, and then for ever!
Deep in heart-wrung tears I'll pledge thee,
Warring sighs and groans I'll wage thee –

Who shall say that Fortune grieves him,
While the star of hope she leaves him:
Me, nae chearful twinkle lights me;
Dark despair around benights me –

I'll ne'er blame my partial fancy,
Naething could resist my Nancy:
But to see her, was to love her;
Love but her, and love for ever –

Had we never lov'd sae kindly,
Had we never lov'd sae blindly!
Never met – or never parted,
We had ne'er been broken hearted –

Fare-thee-weel, thou first and fairest!
Fare-thee-weel thou best and dearest!
Thine be ilka joy and treasure,
Peace, Enjoyment, Love and Pleasure! –

Ae fond kiss and then we sever!
Ae fareweel! Alas, for ever:
Deep in heart-wrung tears I'll pledge thee,
Warring sighs and groans I'll wage thee –

ROBERT BURNS

'O whistle, and I'll come to ye, my lad'

O whistle, and I'll come to ye, my lad,
O whistle, and I'll come to ye, my lad;
Tho' father, and mother, and a' should gae mad,
   Thy Jeanie will venture wi' ye, my lad.

But warily tent, when ye come to court me,
And come nae unless the back-yett be a-jee;
Syne up the back-style and let naebody see,
   And come as ye were na comin to me –
   And come as ye were na comin to me –
      O whistle &c.

At kirk, or at market whene'er ye meet me,
Gang by me as tho' that ye car'd nae a flie;
But steal me a blink o' your bonie black e'e,
   Yet look as ye were na lookin at me –
   Yet look as ye were na lookin at me –
      O whistle &c.

Ay vow and protest that ye care na for me,
And whyles ye may lightly my beauty a wee;
But court nae anither, tho' jokin ye be,
  For fear that she wyle your fancy frae me –
  For fear that she wyle your fancy frae me –

ROBERT BURNS

The Banks o' Doon

Ye banks and braes o' bonie Doon,
  How can ye bloom sae fresh and fair;
How can ye chant, ye little birds,
  And I sae weary fu' o' care!
Thou'll break my heart, thou warbling bird,
  That wantons thro' the flowering thorn:
Thou minds me o' departed joys,
  Departed never to return.

Oft hae I rov'd by bonie Doon,
  To see the rose and woodbine twine
And ilka bird sang o' its luve,
  And fondly sae did I o' mine.
Wi' lightsome heart I pu'd a rose,
  Fu' sweet upon its thorny tree;
And my fause luver staw my rose,
  But ah! he left the thorn wi' me.

ROBERT BURNS

The Solitary Reaper

Behold her, single in the field,
Yon solitary Highland Lass!
Reaping and singing by herself;
Stop here, or gently pass!
Alone she cuts and binds the grain,
And sings a melancholy strain;
O listen! for the Vale profound
Is overflowing with the sound.

No Nightingale did ever chaunt
More welcome notes to weary bands
Of travellers in some shady haunt,
Among Arabian sands:
A voice so thrilling ne'er was heard
In spring-time from the Cuckoo-bird,
Breaking the silence of the seas
Among the farthest Hebrides.

Will no one tell me what she sings? –
Perhaps the plaintive numbers flow
For old, unhappy, far-off things,
And battles long ago:
Or is it some more humble lay,
Familiar matter of today?
Some natural sorrow, loss, or pain,
That has been, and may be again?

Whate'er the theme, the Maiden sang
As if her song could have no ending;
I saw her singing at her work,
And o'er the sickle bending; –
I listened, motionless and still;
And, as I mounted up the hill,
The music in my heart I bore,
Long after it was heard no more.

WILLIAM WORDSWORTH

For a' that and a' that

Is there, for honest Poverty
　　That hings his head, and a' that;
The coward-slave, we pass him by,
　　We dare be poor for a' that!
　For a' that, and a' that,
　　Our toils obscure, and a' that,
　The rank is but the guinea's stamp,
　　The Man's the gowd for a' that –

What though on hamely fare we dine,
　　Wear hoddin grey, and a' that.
Gie fools their silks, and knaves their wine,
　　A Man's a Man for a' that.
　For a' that, and a' that;
　　Their tinsel show, and a' that;
　The honest man, though e'er sae poor,
　　Is king o' men for a' that —

Ye see yon birkie ca'd, a lord,
　　Wha struts, and stares, and a' that,
Though hundreds worship at his word,
　　He's but a coof for a' that.
　For a' that, and a' that,
　　His ribband, star and a' that,
　The man of independant mind,
　　He looks and laughs at a' that —

A prince can mak a belted knight,
　　A marquis, duke, and a' that;
But an honest man's aboon his might,
　　Gude faith he mauna fa' that!
　For a' that, and a' that,
　　Their dignities, and a' that,
　The pith o' Sense, and pride o' Worth,
　　Are higher rank than a' that —

Then let us pray that come it may,
　　As come it will for a' that,
That Sense and Worth, o'er a' the earth
　　Shall bear the gree, and a' that.
　For a' that, and a' that,
　　Its comin yet for a' that,
　That Man to Man the warld o'er,
　　Shall brothers be for a' that —

ROBERT BURNS

Dejection: An Ode

Late, late yestreen I saw the new Moon,
With the old Moon in her arms;
And I fear, I fear, my Master dear!
We shall have a deadly storm.
Ballad of Sir Patrick Spence

Well! If the Bard was weather-wise, who made
   The grand old ballad of Sir Patrick Spence,
   This night, so tranquil now, will not go hence
Unroused by winds, that ply a busier trade
Than those which mould yon cloud in lazy flakes,
Or the dull sobbing draft, that moans and rakes
     Upon the strings of this Æolian lute,
    Which better far were mute.
   For lo! the New-moon winter-bright!
   And overspread with phantom light,
   (With swimming phantom light o'erspread
   But rimmed and circled by a silver thread)
I see the old Moon in her lap, foretelling
   The coming-on of rain and squally blast.
And oh! that even now the gust were swelling,
   And the slant night-shower driving loud and fast!
Those sounds which oft have raised me, whilst they awed,
   And sent my soul abroad,
Might now perhaps their wonted impulse give,
Might startle this dull pain, and make it move and live!

A grief without a pang, void, dark, and drear,
   A stifled, drowsy, unimpassioned grief,
   Which finds no natural outlet, no relief,
     In word, or sigh, or tear –
O Lady! in this wan and heartless mood,
To other thoughts by yonder throstle woo'd,
   All this long eve, so balmy and serene,
Have I been gazing on the western sky,
   And its peculiar tint of yellow green:

And still I gaze – and with how blank an eye!
And those thin clouds above, in flakes and bars,
That give away their motion to the stars;
Those stars, that glide behind them or between,
Now sparkling, now bedimmed, but always seen:
Yon crescent Moon, as fixed as if it grew
In its own cloudless, starless lake of blue;
I see them all so excellently fair,
I see, not feel, how beautiful they are!

    My genial spirits fail;
    And what can these avail
To lift the smothering weight from off my breast?
    It were a vain endeavour,
    Though I should gaze for ever
On that green light that lingers in the west:
I may not hope from outward forms to win
The passion and the life, whose fountains are within.

O Lady! we receive but what we give,
And in our life alone does Nature live:
Ours is her wedding garment, ours her shroud!
    And would we aught behold, of higher worth,
Than that inanimate cold world allowed
To the poor loveless ever-anxious crowd,
    Ah! from the soul itself must issue forth
A light, a glory, a fair luminous cloud
    Enveloping the Earth –
And from the soul itself must there be sent
    A sweet and potent voice, of its own birth,
Of all sweet sounds the life and element!

O pure of heart! thou need'st not ask of me
What this strong music in the soul may be!
What, and wherein it doth exist,
This light, this glory, this fair luminous mist,
This beautiful and beauty-making power.
    Joy, virtuous Lady! Joy that ne'er was given,
Save to the pure, and in their purest hour,
Life, and Life's effluence, cloud at once and shower,

Joy, Lady! is the spirit and the power,
Which wedding Nature to us gives in dower
   A new Earth and new Heaven,
Undreamt of by the sensual and the proud –
Joy is the sweet voice, Joy the luminous cloud –
     We in ourselves rejoice!
And thence flows all that charms or ear or sight,
   All melodies the echoes of that voice,
All colours a suffusion from that light.

There was a time when, though my path was rough,
   This joy within me dallied with distress,
And all misfortunes were but as the stuff
   Whence Fancy made me dreams of happiness:
For hope grew round me, like the twining vine,
And fruits, and foliage, not my own, seemed mine.
But now afflictions bow me down to earth:
Nor care I that they rob me of my mirth;
    But oh! each visitation
Suspends what nature gave me at my birth,
   My shaping spirit of Imagination.
For not to think of what I needs must feel,
   But to be still and patient, all I can;
And haply by abstruse research to steal
   From my own nature all the natural man –
   This was my sole resource, my only plan:
Till that which suits a part infects the whole,
And now is almost grown the habit of my soul.

Hence, viper thoughts, that coil around my mind,
    Reality's dark dream!
I turn from you, and listen to the wind,
   Which long has raved unnoticed. What a scream
Of agony by torture lengthened out
That lute sent forth! Thou Wind, that rav'st without,
   Bare crag, or mountain-tairn, or blasted tree,
Or pine-grove whither woodman never clomb,
Or lonely house, long held the witches' home,
   Methinks were fitter instruments for thee,
Mad Lutanist! who in this month of showers,

Of dark-brown gardens, and of peeping flowers,
Mak'st Devils' yule, with worse than wintry song,
The blossoms, buds, and timorous leaves among.
    Thou Actor, perfect in all tragic sounds!
Thou mighty Poet, e'en to frenzy bold!
      What tell'st thou now about?
      'Tis of the rushing of an host in rout,
   With groans, of trampled men, with smarting wounds –
At once they groan with pain, and shudder with the cold!
But hush! there is a pause of deepest silence!
    And all that noise, as of a rushing crowd,
With groans, and tremulous shudderings – all is over –
   It tells another tale, with sounds less deep and loud!
      A tale of less affright,
      And tempered with delight,
As Otway's self had framed the tender lay, –
      'Tis of a little child
      Upon a lonesome wild,
Not far from home, but she hath lost her way:
And now moans low in bitter grief and fear,
And now screams loud, and hopes to make her mother hear.

'Tis midnight, but small thoughts have I of sleep:
Full seldom may my friend such vigils keep!
Visit her, gentle Sleep! with wings of healing,
    And may this storm be but a mountain-birth,
May all the stars hang bright above her dwelling,
   Silent as though they watched the sleeping Earth!
      With light heart may she rise,
      Gay fancy, cheerful eyes,
   Joy lift her spirit, joy attune her voice;
To her may all things live, from pole to pole,
Their life the eddying of her living soul!
    O simple spirit, guided from above,
Dear Lady! friend devoutest of my choice,
Thus mayest thou ever, evermore rejoice.

SAMUEL TAYLOR COLERIDGE

Ah! Sun-flower

Ah Sun-flower! weary of time.
Who countest the steps of the Sun:
Seeking after that sweet golden clime
Where the travellers journey is done.

Where the Youth pined away with desire,
And the pale Virgin shrouded in snow:
Arise from their graves and aspire,
Where my Sun-flower wishes to go.

WILLIAM BLAKE

To a Butterfly

I've watched you now a full half-hour,
Self-poised upon that yellow flower;
And, little Butterfly! indeed
I know not if you sleep or feed.
How motionless! – not frozen seas
More motionless! and then
What joy awaits you, when the breeze
Hath found you out among the trees,
And calls you forth again!

This plot of orchard-ground is ours;
My trees they are, my Sister's flowers;
Here rest your wings when they are weary;
Here lodge as in a sanctuary!
Come often to us, fear no wrong;
Sit near us on the bough!
We'll talk of sunshine and of song,
And summer days, when we were young;
Sweet childish days, that were as long
As twenty days are now.

WILLIAM WORDSWORTH

'Strange fits of passion have I known'

Strange fits of passion have I known:
And I will dare to tell,
But in the Lover's ear alone,
What once to me befell.

When she I loved looked every day
Fresh as a rose in June,
I to her cottage bent my way,
Beneath an evening moon.

Upon the moon I fixed my eye,
All over the wide lea;
With quickening pace my horse drew nigh
Those paths so dear to me.

And now we reached the orchard-plot;
And, as we climbed the hill,
The sinking moon to Lucy's cot
Came near, and nearer still.

In one of those sweet dreams I slept,
Kind Nature's gentlest boon!
And all the while my eyes I kept
On the descending moon.

My horse moved on; hoof after hoof
He raised, and never stopped:
When down behind the cottage roof,
At once, the bright moon dropped.

What fond and wayward thoughts will slide
Into a Lover's head!
'O mercy!' to myself I cried,
'If Lucy should be dead!'

WILLIAM WORDSWORTH

'She walks in beauty'

She walks in Beauty, like the night
    Of cloudless climes and starry skies;
And all that's best of dark and bright
    Meet in her aspect and her eyes:
Thus mellowed to that tender light
    Which Heaven to gaudy day denies.

One shade the more, one ray the less,
    Had half impaired the nameless grace
Which waves in every raven tress,
    Or softly lightens o'er her face;
Where thoughts serenely sweet express,
    How pure, how dear their dwelling-place.

And on that cheek, and o'er that brow,
    So soft, so calm, yet eloquent,
The smiles that win, the tints that glow,
    But tell of days in goodness spent,
A mind at peace with all below,
    A heart whose love is innocent!

LORD BYRON

Stanzas for Music

There be none of Beauty's daughters
    With a magic like thee;
And like music on the waters
    Is thy sweet voice to me:
When, as if its sound were causing
The charméd Ocean's pausing
The waves lie still and gleaming,
And the lulled winds seem dreaming:

And the Midnight Moon is weaving
    Her bright chain o'er the deep;
Whose breast is gently heaving,

As an infant's asleep:
So the spirit bows before thee,
To listen and adore thee,
With a full but soft emotion,
Like the swell of Summer's ocean.

LORD BYRON

'She dwelt among the untrodden ways'

She dwelt among the untrodden ways
    Beside the springs of Dove,
A Maid whom there were none to praise
    And very few to love:

A violet by a mossy stone
    Half hidden from the eye!
— Fair as a star, when only one
    Is shining in the sky.

She lived unknown, and few could know
    When Lucy ceased to be;
But she is in her grave, and, oh,
    The difference to me!

WILLIAM WORDSWORTH

'A slumber did my spirit seal'

A slumber did my spirit seal;
    I had no human fears:
She seemed a thing that could not feel
    The touch of earthly years.

No motion has she now, no force;
    She neither hears nor sees;
Rolled round in earth's diurnal course,
    With rocks, and stones, and trees.

WILLIAM WORDSWORTH

Ozymandias

I met a traveller from an antique land
Who said: Two vast and trunkless legs of stone
Stand in the desert . . . Near them, on the sand,
Half sunk, a shattered visage lies, whose frown,
And wrinkled lip, and sneer of cold command,
Tell that its sculptor well those passions read
Which yet survive, stamped on these lifeless things,
The hand that mocked them, and the heart that fed:
And on the pedestal these words appear:
'My name is Ozymandias, king of kings:
Look on my works, ye Mighty, and despair!'
Nothing beside remains. Round the decay
Of that colossal wreck, boundless and bare
The lone and level sands stretch far away.

PERCY BYSSHE SHELLEY

Ode to the West Wind

I

O wild West Wind, thou breath of Autumn's being,
    Thou from whose unseen presence the leaves dead
Are driven like ghosts from an enchanter fleeing,
    Yellow, and black, and pale, and hectic red,
Pestilence-stricken multitudes! O thou
    Who chariotest to their dark wintry bed

The wingèd seeds, where they lie cold and low,
    Each like a corpse within its grave, until
Thine azure sister of the Spring shall blow

    Her clarion o'er the dreaming earth, and fill
(Driving sweet buds like flocks to feed in air)
    With living hues and odours plain and hill;

Wild Spirit, which art moving everywhere;
Destroyer and preserver; hear, O hear!

II

Thou on whose stream, mid the steep sky's commotion,
    Loose clouds like earth's decaying leaves are shed,
Shook from the tangled boughs of heaven and ocean,

    Angels of rain and lightning! there are spread
On the blue surface of thine airy surge,
    Like the bright hair uplifted from the head

Of some fierce Maenad, even from the dim verge
    Of the horizon to the zenith's height,
The locks of the approaching storm. Thou dirge

    Of the dying year, to which this closing night
Will be the dome of a vast sepulchre,
    Vaulted with all thy congregated might

Of vapours, from whose solid atmosphere
Black rain, and fire, and hail will burst: O hear!

III

Thou who didst waken from his summer dreams
    The blue Mediterranean, where he lay,
Lulled by the coil of his crystalline streams,

    Beside a pumice isle in Baiae's bay,
And saw in sleep old palaces and towers
    Quivering within the wave's intenser day,

All overgrown with azure moss, and flowers
    So sweet, the sense faints picturing them! Thou
For whose path the Atlantic's level powers

    Cleave themselves into chasms, while far below
The sea-blooms and the oozy woods which wear
    The sapless foliage of the ocean, know

Thy voice, and suddenly grow gray with fear,
And tremble and despoil themselves: O hear!

IV

If I were a dead leaf thou mightest bear;
   If I were a swift cloud to fly with thee;
A wave to pant beneath thy power, and share

   The impulse of thy strength, only less free
Than thou, O uncontrollable! if even
   I were as in my boyhood, and could be

The comrade of thy wanderings over heaven,
   As then, when to outstrip thy skiey speed
Scarce seemed a vision – I would ne'er have striven

   As thus with thee in prayer in my sore need.
O! lift me as a wave, a leaf, a cloud!
   I fall upon the thorns of life! I bleed!

A heavy weight of hours has chained and bowed
One too like thee – tameless, and swift, and proud.

V

Make me thy lyre, even as the forest is:
   What if my leaves are falling like its own?
The tumult of thy mighty harmonies

   Will take from both a deep autumnal tone,
Sweet though in sadness. Be thou, Spirit fierce,
   My spirit! Be thou me, impetuous one!

Drive my dead thoughts over the universe,
   Like withered leaves, to quicken a new birth;
And, by the incantation of this verse,

   Scatter, as from an unextinguished hearth
Ashes and sparks, my words among mankind!
   Be through my lips to unawakened earth

The trumpet of a prophecy! O Wind,
If Winter comes, can Spring be far behind?

PERCY BYSSHE SHELLEY

Kubla Khan

In Xanadu did Kubla Khan
A stately pleasure-dome decree:
Where Alph, the sacred river, ran
Through caverns measureless to man
   Down to a sunless sea.
So twice five miles of fertile ground
With walls and towers were girdled round:
And there were gardens bright with sinuous rills,
Where blossomed many an incense-bearing tree;
And here were forests ancient as the hills,
Enfolding sunny spots of greenery.

But oh! that deep romantic chasm which slanted
Down the green hill athwart a cedarn cover!
A savage place! as holy and enchanted
As e'er beneath a waning moon was haunted
By woman wailing for her demon-lover!
And from this chasm, with ceaseless turmoil seething,
As if this earth in fast thick pants were breathing,
A mighty fountain momently was forced:
Amid whose swift half-intermitted burst
Huge fragments vaulted like rebounding hail,
Or chaffy grain beneath the thresher's flail:
And 'mid these dancing rocks at once and ever
It flung up momently the sacred river.
Five miles meandering with a mazy motion
Through wood and dale the sacred river ran,
Then reached the caverns measureless to man,
And sank in tumult to a lifeless ocean:
And 'mid this tumult Kubla heard from far
Ancestral voices prophesying war!
   The shadow of the dome of pleasure
   Floated midway on the waves;
   Where was heard the mingled measure
   From the fountain and the caves.

It was a miracle of rare device,
A sunny pleasure-dome with caves of ice!

A damsel with a dulcimer
In a vision once I saw:
It was an Abyssinian maid,
And on her dulcimer she played,
Singing of Mount Abora.
Could I revive *within* me
Her symphony and song,
To such a deep delight 'twould win me,
That with music *loud* and long,
I would build that dome in air,
That sunny dome! those caves of ice!
And all who heard should see them there,
And all should cry, Beware! Beware!
His flashing eyes, his floating hair!
Weave a circle round him thrice,
And close your eyes with holy dread,
For he on honey-dew hath fed,
And drunk the milk of Paradise.

SAMUEL TAYLOR COLERIDGE

An Answer to the Parson

Why of the sheep do you not learn peace?
'Because I don't want you to shear my fleece.'

ANON

Sonnet: England in 1819

An old, mad, blind, despised, and dying king, –
Princes, the dregs of their dull race, who flow
Through public scorn, – mud from a muddy spring, –
Rulers who neither see, nor feel, nor know,
But leechlike to their fainting country cling,
Till they drop, blind in blood, without a blow, –
A people starved and stabbed in the untilled field, –

An army, which liberticide and prey
Makes as a two-edged sword to all who wield, –
Golden and sanguine laws which tempt and slay;
Religion Christless, Godless – a book sealed;
A Senate, – Time's worst statute unrepealed, –
Are graves, from which a glorious Phantom may
Burst, to illumine our tempestuous day.

PERCY BYSSHE SHELLEY

The Destruction of Sennacherib

The Assyrian came down like the wolf on the fold,
And his cohorts were gleaming in purple and gold;
And the sheen of their spears was like stars on the sea,
When the blue wave rolls nightly on deep Galilee.

Like the leaves of the forest when Summer is green,
That host with their banners at sunset were seen:
Like the leaves of the forest when Autumn hath blown,
That host on the morrow lay withered and strown.

For the Angel of Death spread his wings on the blast,
And breathed in the face of the foe as he passed;
And the eyes of the sleepers waxed deadly and chill,
And their hearts but once heaved, and for ever grew still.

And there lay the steed with his nostril all wide,
But through it there rolled not the breath of his pride:
And the foam of his gasping lay white on the turf,
And cold as the spray of the rock-beating surf.

And there lay the rider distorted and pale,
With the dew on his brow and the rust on his mail;
And the tents were all silent, the banners alone,
The lances unlifted, the trumpet unblown.

And the widows of Ashur are loud in their wail,
And the idols are broke in the temple of Baal:
And the might of the Gentile, unsmote by the sword,
Hath melted like snow in the glance of the Lord!

LORD BYRON

Lines

When the lamp is shatter'd,
The light in the dust lies dead;
   When the cloud is scatter'd,
The rainbow's glory is shed:
   When the lute is broken,
Sweet tones are remember'd not
   When the lips have spoken,
Loved accents are soon forgot.

   As music and splendour
Survive not the lamp and the lute,
   The heart's echoes render
No song when the spirit is mute –
   No song but sad dirges,
Like the wind through a ruin'd cell,
   Or the mournful surges
That ring the dead seaman's knell.

   When hearts have once mingled,
Love first leaves the well-built nest;
   The weak one is singled
To endure what it once possest.
   O Love, who bewailest
The frailty of all things here,
   Why choose you the frailest
For your cradle, your home, and your bier?

   Its passions will rock thee,
As the storms rock the ravens on high;
   Bright reason will mock thee,
Like the sun from a wintry sky.
   From thy nest every rafter
Will rot, and thine eagle home
   Leave thee naked to laughter,
When leaves fall and cold winds come.

PERCY BYSSHE SHELLEY

'Remember thee! remember thee!'

Remember thee! remember thee!
    Till Lethe quench Life's burning stream
Remorse and Shame shall cling to thee,
    And haunt thee like a feverish dream!
Remember thee! Aye, doubt it not.
    Thy husband too shall think of thee:
By neither shalt thou be forgot,
    Thou *false* to him, thou *fiend* to me!

LORD BYRON

Hellas

The world's great age begins anew,
    The golden years return,
The earth doth like a snake renew
    Her winter weeds outworn:
Heaven smiles, and faiths and empires gleam,
Like wrecks of a dissolving dream.

A brighter Hellas rears its mountains
    From waves serener far;
A new Peneus rolls his fountains
    Against the morning star.
Where fairer Tempes bloom, there sleep
Young Cyclads on a sunnier deep.

A loftier Argo cleaves the main,
    Fraught with a later prize;
Another Orpheus sings again,
    And loves, and weeps, and dies.
A new Ulysses leaves once more
Calypso for his native shore.

Oh, write no more the tale of Troy,
    If earth Death's scroll must be!
Nor mix with Laian rage the joy
    Which dawns upon the free:
Although a subtler Sphinx renew
Riddles of death Thebes never knew.

Another Athens shall arise,
    And to remoter time
Bequeath, like sunset to the skies,
    The splendour of its prime;
And leave, if nought so bright may live,
All earth can take or Heaven can give.

Saturn and Love their long repose
    Shall burst, more bright and good
Than all who fell, than One who rose,
    Than many unsubdued:
Not gold, not blood, their altar dowers,
But votive tears and symbol flowers.

Oh, cease! must hate and death return?
    Cease! must men kill and die?
Cease! drain not to its dregs the urn
    Of bitter prophecy.
The world is weary of the past,
Oh, might it die or rest at last!

PERCY BYSSHE SHELLEY

'When we two parted'

When we two parted
    In silence and tears,
Half broken-hearted
    To sever for years,
Pale grew thy cheek and cold,
    Colder thy kiss;
Truly that hour foretold
    Sorrow to this.

The dew of the morning
   Sunk chill on my brow –
It felt like the warning
   Of what I feel now.
Thy vows are all broken,
   And light is thy fame;
I hear thy name spoken,
   And share in its shame.

They name thee before me,
   A knell to mine ear;
A shudder comes o'er me –
   Why wert thou so dear?
They know not I knew thee,
   Who knew thee too well: –
Long, long shall I rue thee,
   Too deeply to tell.

In secret we met –
   In silence I grieve,
That thy heart could forget,
   Thy spirit deceive.
If I should meet thee
   After long years,
How should I greet thee? –
   With silence and tears.

LORD BYRON

To a Skylark

Hail to thee, blithe Spirit
   Bird thou never wert,
That from Heaven, or near it,
   Pourest thy full heart
In profuse strains of unpremeditated art.

Higher still and higher
   From the earth thou springest
Like a cloud of fire;

The blue deep thou wingest,
And singing still dost soar, and soaring ever singest.

In the golden lightning
    Of the sunken sun,
O'er which clouds are bright'ning,
    Thou dost float and run;
Like an unbodied joy whose race is just begun.

The pale purple even
    Melts around thy flight;
Like a star of Heaven,
    In the broad daylight
Thou art unseen, but yet I hear thy shrill delight,

Keen as are the arrows
    Of that silver sphere,
Whose intense lamp narrows
    In the white dawn clear
Until we hardly see — we feel that it is there.

All the earth and air
    With thy voice is loud,
As, when night is bare,
    From one lonely cloud
The moon rains out her beams, and Heaven is over-flowed.

What thou art we know not;
    What is most like thee?
From rainbow clouds there flow not
    Drops so bright to see
As from thy presence showers a rain of melody.

Like a Poet hidden
    In the light of thought,
Singing hymns unbidden,
    Till the world is wrought
To sympathy with hopes and fears it heeded not:

Like a high-born maiden
    In a palace-tower,
Soothing her love-laden

Soul in secret hour
With music sweet as love, which overflows her bower:

Like a glow-worm golden
    In a dell of dew,
Scattering unbeholden
    Its aëreal hue
Among the flowers and grass, which screen it from the view!

Like a rose embowered
    In its own green leaves,
By warm winds deflowered,
    Till the scent it gives
Makes faint with too much sweet those heavy-wingèd thieves:

Sound of vernal showers
    On the twinkling grass,
Rain-awakened flowers,
    All that ever was
Joyous, and clear, and fresh, thy music doth surpass:

Teach us, Sprite or Bird,
    What sweet thoughts are thine:
I have never heard
    Praise of love or wine
That panted forth a flood of rapture so divine.

Chorus Hymeneal,
    Or triumphal chant,
Matched with thine would be all
    But an empty vaunt,
A thing wherein we feel there is some hidden want.

What objects are the fountains
    Of thy happy strain?
What fields, or waves, or mountains?
    What shapes of sky or plain?
What love of thine own kind? what ignorance of pain?

With thy clear keen joyance
    Languor cannot be:
Shadow of annoyance

Never came near thee:
Thou lovest – but ne'er knew love's sad satiety.

Waking or asleep,
    Thou of death must deem
Things more true and deep
    Than we mortals dream,
Or how could thy notes flow in such a crystal stream?

We look before and after,
    And pine for what is not:
Our sincerest laughter
    With some pain is fraught;
Our sweetest songs are those that tell of saddest thought.

Yet if we could scorn
    Hate, and pride, and fear;
If we were things born
    Not to shed a tear,
I know not how thy joy we ever should come near.

Better than all measures
    Of delightful sound,
Better than all treasures
    That in books are found,
Thy skill to poet were, thou scorner of the ground!

Teach me half the gladness
    That thy brain must know,
Such harmonious madness
    From my lips would flow
The world should listen then – as I am listening now.

PERCY BYSSHE SHELLEY

Stanzas

WRITTEN IN DEJECTION, NEAR NAPLES

The sun is warm, the sky is clear,
    The waves are dancing fast and bright,
Blue isles and snowy mountains wear

The purple noon's transparent might,
    The breath of the moist earth is light,
Around its unexpanded buds;
    Like many a voice of one delight,
The winds, the birds, the ocean floods,
The City's voice itself, is soft like Solitude's.

I see the Deep's untrampled floor
    With green and purple seaweeds strown;
I see the waves upon the shore,
    Like light dissolved in star-showers, thrown:
    I sit upon the sands alone, –
The lightning of the noontide ocean
    Is flashing round me, and a tone
Arises from its measured motion,
How sweet! did any heart now share in my emotion.

Alas! I have nor hope nor health,
    Nor peace within nor calm around,
Nor that content surpassing wealth
    The sage in meditation found,
    And walked with inward glory crowned –
Nor fame, nor power, nor love, nor leisure.
    Others I see whom these surround –
Smiling they live, and call life pleasure; –
To me that cup has been dealt in another measure.

Yet now despair itself is mild,
    Even as the winds and waters are;
I could lie down like a tired child,
    And weep away the life of care
    Which I have borne and yet must bear,
Till death like sleep might steal on me,
    And I might feel in the warm air
My cheek grow cold, and hear the sea
Breathe o'er my dying brain its last monotony.

Some might lament that I were cold,
    As I, when this sweet day is gone,
Which my lost heart, too soon grown old,
    Insults with this untimely moan;

They might lament – for I am one
Whom men love not, – and yet regret,
Unlike this day, which, when the sun
Shall on its stainless glory set,
Will linger, though enjoyed, like joy in memory yet.

PERCY BYSSHE SHELLEY

The Mask of Anarchy

As I lay asleep in Italy
There came a voice from over the Sea,
And with great power it forth led me
To walk in the visions of Poesy.

I met Murder on the way –
He had a mask like Castlereagh –
Very smooth he looked, yet grim;
Seven blood-hounds followed him:

All were fat; and well they might
Be in admirable plight,
For one by one, and two by two,
He tossed them human hearts to chew
Which from his wide cloak he drew.

Next came Fraud, and he had on,
Like Eldon, an ermined gown;
His big tears, for he wept well,
Turned to mill-stones as they fell.

And the little children, who
Round his feet played to and fro,
Thinking every tear a gem,
Had their brains knocked out by them.

Clothed with the Bible, as with light,
And the shadows of the night,
Like Sidmouth, next, Hypocrisy
On a crocodile rode by.

And many more Destructions played
In this ghastly masquerade,
All disguised, even to the eyes,
Like Bishops, lawyers, peers, or spies.

Last came Anarchy: he rode
On a white horse, splashed with blood;
He was pale even to the lips,
Like Death in the Apocalypse.

And he wore a kingly crown;
And in his grasp a sceptre shone;
On his brow this mark I saw –
'I AM GOD, AND KING, AND LAW!'

With a pace stately and fast,
Over English land he passed,
Trampling to a mire of blood
The adoring multitude.

And a mighty troop around,
With their trampling shook the ground,
Waving each a bloody sword,
For the service of their Lord.

And with glorious triumph, they
Rode through England proud and gay,
Drunk as with intoxication
Of the wine of desolation.

O'er fields and towns, from sea to sea,
Passed the Pageant swift and free,
Tearing up, and trampling down;
Till they came to London town.

And each dweller, panic-stricken,
Felt his heart with terror sicken
Hearing the tempestuous cry
Of the triumph of Anarchy.

For with pomp to meet him came,
Clothed in arms like blood and flame,

The hired murderers, who did sing
'Thou art God, and Law, and King.'

'There was a boy'

There was a boy; ye knew him well, ye cliffs
And islands of Winander! – many a time,
At evening when the earliest stars began
To move along the edges of the hills,
Rising or setting, would he stand alone,
Beneath the trees, or by the glimmering lake;
And there, with fingers interwoven, both hands
Pressed closely palm to palm and to his mouth
Uplifted, he, as through an instrument,
Blew mimic hootings to the silent owls,
That they might answer him. – And they would shout
Across the watery vale, and shout again,
Responsive to his call, – with quivering peals,
And long halloos, and screams, and echoes loud
Redoubled and redoubled; concourse wild
Of jocund din! And, when there came a pause
Of silence such as baffled his best skill:
Then, sometimes, in that silence, while he hung
Listening, a gentle shock of mild surprise
Has carried far into his heart the voice
Of mountain-torrents; or the visible scene
Would enter unawares into his mind
With all its solemn imagery, its rocks,
Its woods, and that uncertain heaven received
Into the bosom of the steady lake.
This boy was taken from his mates, and died
In childhood, ere he was full twelve years old.
Pre-eminent in beauty is the vale
Where he was born and bred: the churchyard hangs
Upon a slope above the village-school;
And, through that churchyard when my way has led
On summer-evenings, I believe, that there

A long half-hour together I have stood
Mute – looking at the grave in which he lies!

WILLIAM WORDSWORTH

To a Skylark

Ethereal minstrel! pilgrim of the sky!
Dost thou despise the earth where cares abound?
Or, while the wings aspire, are heart and eye
Both with thy nest upon the dewy ground?
Thy nest which thou canst drop into at will,
Those quivering wings composed, that music still!

Leave to the nightingale her shady wood;
A privacy of glorious light is thine;
Whence thou dost pour upon the world a flood
Of harmony, with instinct more divine;
Type of the wise who soar, but never roam;
True to the kindred points of Heaven and Home!

WILLIAM WORDSWORTH

The Netherlands

Water and windmills, greenness, Islets green; –
Willows whose Trunks beside the shadows stood
Of their own higher half, and willowy swamp: –
Farmhouses that at anchor seem'd – in the inland sky
The fog-transfixing Spires –
Water, wide water, greenness and green banks,
And water seen –

SAMUEL TAYLOR COLERIDGE

'Great things are done'

Great things are done when men and mountains meet:
This is not done by jostling in the street.

ANON.

The Cloud

I bring fresh showers for the thirsting flowers,
    From the seas and the streams;
I bear light shade for the leaves when laid
      In their noonday dreams.
From my wings are shaken the dews that waken
      The sweet buds every one,
When rocked to rest on their mother's breast,
      As she dances about the sun.
I wield the flail of the lashing hail,
      And whiten the green plains under,
And then again I dissolve it in rain,
      And laugh as I pass in thunder.

I sift the snow on the mountains below,
      And their great pines groan aghast;
And all the night 'tis my pillow white,
      While I sleep in the arms of the blast.
Sublime on the towers of my skiey bowers,
      Lightning my pilot sits;
In a cavern under is fettered the thunder,
      It struggles and howls at fits;
Over earth and ocean, with gentle motion,
      This pilot is guiding me,
Lured by the love of the genii that move
      In the depths of the purple sea;
Over the rills, and the crags, and the hills,
      Over the lakes and the plains,
Wherever he dream, under mountain or stream,
      The Spirit he loves remains;

And I all the while bask in Heaven's blue smile,
      Whilst he is dissolving in rains.

The sanguine Sunrise, with the meteor eyes,
      And his burning plumes outspread,
Leaps on the back of my sailing rack,
      When the morning star shines dead:
As on the jag of a mountain crag,
      Which an earthquake rocks and swings,
An eagle alit one moment may sit
      In the light of its golden wings.
And when Sunset may breathe, from the lit sea beneath,
      It ardours of rest and of love,
And the crimson pall of eve may fall
      from the depth of Heaven above,
With wings folded I rest, on mine aëry nest,
      As still as a brooding dove.

That orbèd maiden with white fire laden,
      Whom mortals call the Moon,
Glides glimmering o'er my fleece-like floor,
      By the midnight breezes strewn;
And wherever the beat of her unseen feet,
      Which only the angels hear,
May have broken the woof of my tent's thin roof,
      The stars peep behind her and peer;
And I laugh to see them whirl and flee,
      Like a swarm of golden bees,
When I widen the rent in my wind-built tent,
      Till the calm rivers, lakes, and seas,
Like strips of the sky fallen through me on high,
      Are each paved with the moon and these.

I bind the Sun's throne with a burning zone,
      And the Moon's with a girdle of pearl;
The volcanoes are dim, and the stars reel and swim,
      When the whirlwinds my banner unfurl.
From cape to cape, with a bridge-like shape,
      Over a torrent sea,

Sunbeam-proof, I hand like a roof, –
　　The mountains its columns be.
The triumphal arch through which I march
　　With hurricane, fire, and snow,
When the Powers of the air are chained to my chair,
　　Is the million-coloured bow;
The sphere-fire above its soft colours wove,
　　While the moist Earth was laughing below.

I am the daughter of Earth and Water,
　　And the nursling of the Sky;
I pass through the pores of the ocean and shores;
　　I change, but I cannot die.
For after the rain when with never a stain
　　The pavilion of Heaven is bare,
And the winds and sunbeams with their convex gleams
　　Build up the blue dome of air,
I silently laugh at my own cenotaph,
　　And out of the caverns of rain,
Like a child from the womb, like a ghost from the tomb,
　　I arise and unbuild it again.

PERCY BYSSHE SHELLEY

'The spell is broke, the charm is flown'

The spell is broke, the charm is flown!
　　Thus is it with life's fitful fever:
We madly smile when we should groan;
　　Delirium is our best deceiver.

Each lucid interval of thought
　　Recalls the woes of Nature's charter;
And he that acts as wise men ought,
　　But lives, as saints have died, a martyr.

LORD BYRON

La Belle Dame sans Merci: A Ballad

O what can ail thee, knight-at-arms,
　　Alone and palely loitering?
The sedge has withered from the lake,
　　And no birds sing.

O what can ail thee, knight-at-arms,
　　So haggard and so woe-begone?
The squirrel's granary is full,
　　And the harvest's done.

I see a lily on thy brow,
　　With anguish moist and fever-dew,
And on thy cheeks a fading rose
　　Fast withereth too.

I met a lady in the meads,
　　Full beautiful – a faery's child,
Her hair was long, her foot was light,
　　And her eyes were wild.

I made a garland for her head,
　　And bracelets too, and fragrant zone;
She looked at me as she did love,
　　And made sweet moan.

I set her on my pacing steed,
　　And nothing else saw all day long,
For sidelong would she bend, and sing
　　A faery's song.

She found me roots of relish sweet,
　　And honey wild, and manna-dew,
And sure in language strange she said –
　　'I love thee true'.

She took me to her elfin grot,
　　And there she wept and sighed full sore,
And there I shut her wild wild eyes
　　With kisses four.

And there she lullèd me asleep
   And there I dreamed – Ah! woe betide! –
The latest dream I ever dreamt
   On the cold hill side.

I saw pale kings and princes too,
   Pale warriors, death-pale were they all;
They cried – 'La Belle Dame sans Merci
   Thee hath in thrall!'

I saw their starved lips in the gloam,
   With horrid warning gapèd wide,
And I awoke and found me here,
   On the cold hill's side.

And this is why I sojourn here
   Alone and palely loitering,
Though the sedge is withered from the lake,
   And no birds sing.

JOHN KEATS

'So we'll go no more a-roving'

So we'll go no more a-roving
   So late into the night,
Though the heart be still as loving,
   And the moon be still as bright.

For the sword outwears its sheath,
   And the soul wears out the breast,
And the heart must pause to breathe,
   And love itself have rest.

Though the night was made for loving,
   And the day returns too soon,
Yet we'll go no more a-roving
   By the light of the moon.

LORD BYRON

Song

A widow bird sate mourning for her love
    Upon a wintry bough;
The frozen wind crept on above,
    The freezing stream below.

There was no leaf upon the forest bare,
    No flower upon the ground,
And little motion in the air
    Except the mill-wheel's sound.

PERCY BYSSHE SHELLEY

Ode to a Nightingale

My heart aches, and a drowsy numbness pains
    My sense, as though of hemlock I had drunk,
Or emptied some dull opiate to the drains
    One minute past, and Lethe-wards had sunk:
'Tis not through envy of thy happy lot,
    But being too happy in thine happiness –
        That thou, light-wingèd Dryad of the trees,
        In some melodious plot
Of beechen green, and shadows numberless,
    Singest of summer in full-throated ease.

O, for a draught of vintage! that hath been
    Cooled a long age in the deep-delvèd earth,
Tasting of Flora and the country green,
    Dance, and Provençal song, and sunburnt mirth!
O for a beaker full of the warm South,
    Full of the true, the blushful Hippocrene,
        With beaded bubbles winking at the brim,
        And purple-stainèd mouth,
That I might drink, and leave the world unseen,
    And with thee fade away into the forest dim –

Fade far away, dissolve, and quite forget
    What thou among the leaves hast never known,

The weariness, the fever, and the fret
   Here, where men sit and hear each other groan;
Where palsy shakes a few, sad, last grey hairs,
    Where youth grows pale, and spectre-thin, and dies;
      Where but to think is to be full of sorrow
        And leaden-eyed despairs;
Where Beauty cannot keep her lustrous eyes,
   Or new Love pine at them beyond to-morrow.

Away! away! for I will fly to thee,
   Not charioted by Bacchus and his pards,
But on the viewless wings of Poesy,
   Though the dull brain perplexes and retards.
Already with thee! tender is the night,
    And haply the Queen-Moon is on her throne,
      Clustered around by all her starry Fays;
        But here there is no light,
   Save what from heaven is with the breezes blown
      Through verdurous glooms and winding mossy ways.

I cannot see what flowers are at my feet,
   Nor what soft incense hangs upon the boughs,
But, in embalmèd darkness, guess each sweet
   Wherewith the seasonable month endows
The grass, the thicket, and the fruit-tree wild –
    White hawthorn, and the pastoral eglantine;
      Fast fading violets covered up in leaves;
        And mid-May's eldest child,
The coming musk-rose, full of dewy wine,
   The murmurous haunt of flies on summer eves.

Darkling I listen; and, for many a time
   I have been half in love with easeful Death,
Called him soft names in many a musèd rhyme,
   To take into the air my quiet breath;
Now more than ever seems it rich to die,
   To cease upon the midnight with no pain,
      While thou art pouring forth thy soul abroad
        In such an ecstasy!

Still wouldst thou sing, and I have ears in vain –
    To thy high requiem become a sod.

Thou wast not born for death, immortal Bird!
    No hungry generations tread thee down;
The voice I hear this passing night was heard
    In ancient days by emperor and clown:
Perhaps the self-same song that found a path
    Through the sad heart of Ruth, when, sick for home,
        She stood in tears amid the alien corn;
            The same that oft-times hath
    Charmed magic casements, opening on the foam
    Of perilous seas, in faery lands forlorn.

Forlorn! the very word is like a bell
    To toll me back from thee to my sole self!
Adieu! the fancy cannot cheat so well
    As she is famed to do, deceiving elf.
Adieu! adieu! thy plaintive anthem fades
    Past the near meadows, over the still stream,
        Up the hill-side; and now 'tis buried deep
            In the next valley-glades:
    Was it a vision, or a waking dream?
        Fled is that music – Do I wake or sleep?

JOHN KEATS

Verse

Past ruin'd Ilion Helen lives,
    Alcestis rises from the shades;
Verse calls them forth; 'tis verse that gives
    Immortal youth to mortal maids.

Soon shall Oblivion's deepening veil
    Hide all the peopled hills you see,
The gay, the proud, while lovers hail
    These many summers you and me.

WALTER SAVAGE LANDOR

Cologne

In Köhln, a town of monks and bones,
And pavements fang'd with murderous stones
And rags, and hags, and hideous wenches;
I counted two and seventy stenches,
All well defined, and several stinks!
Ye Nymphs that reign o'er sewers and sinks,
The river Rhine, it is well known,
Doth wash your city of Cologne;
But tell me, Nymphs, what power divine
Shall henceforth wash the river Rhine?

SAMUEL TAYLOR COLERIDGE

Song to the Men of England

Men of England, wherefore plough
For the lords who lay ye low?
Wherefore weave with toil and care
The rich robes your tyrants wear?

Wherefore feed, and clothe, and save,
From the cradle to the grave,
Those ungrateful drones who would
Drain your sweat – nay, drink your blood?

Wherefore, Bees of England, forge
Many a weapon, chain and scourge,
That these stingless drones may spoil
The forced produce of your toil?

Have ye leisure, comfort, calm,
Shelter, food, love's gentle balm?
Or what is it ye buy so dear
With your pain and with your fear?

The seed ye sow, another reaps:
The wealth ye find, another keeps;
The robes ye weave, another wears;
The arms ye forge, another bears.

Sow seed, – but let no tyrant reap;
Find wealth, – let no imposter heap;
Weaves robes, – let not the idle wear;
Forge arms, – in your defence to bear.

Shrink to your cellars, holes, and cells;
In halls ye deck another dwells.
Why shake the chains ye wrought? Ye see
The steel ye tempered glance on ye.

With plough and spade, and hoe and loom,
Trace your grave and build your tomb,
And weave your winding-sheet, till fair
England be your sepulchre.

PERCY BYSSHE SHELLEY

*Lines Composed a Few Miles above Tintern Abbey,
on Revisiting the Banks of the Wye during a Tour.
July 13, 1798*

Five years have past; five summers, with the length
Of five long winters! and again I hear
These waters, rolling from their mountain-springs
With a soft inland murmur. – Once again
Do I behold these steep and lofty cliffs,
That on a wild secluded scene impress
Thoughts of more deep seclusion; and connect
The landscape with the quiet of the sky.
The day is come when I again repose
Here, under this dark sycamore, and view
These plots of cottage-ground, these orchard-tufts,
Which at this season, with their unripe fruits,
Are clad in one green hue, and lose themselves
'Mid groves and copses. Once again I see
These hedge-rows, hardly hedge-rows, little lines
Of sportive wood run wild: these pastoral farms,
Green to the very door; and wreaths of smoke
Sent up, in silence, from among the trees!
With some uncertain notice, as might seem
Of vagrant dwellers in the houseless woods,

Or of some Hermit's cave, where by his fire
The Hermit sits alone.
                         These beauteous forms,
Through a long absence, have not been to me
As is a landscape to a blind man's eye:
But oft, in lonely rooms, and 'mid the din
Of towns and cities, I have owed to them
In hours of weariness, sensations sweet,
Felt in the blood, and felt along the heart;
And passing even into my purer mind,
With tranquil restoration: – feelings too
Of unremembered pleasure: such, perhaps,
As have no slight or trivial influence
On that best portion of a good man's life,
His little, nameless, unremembered, acts
Of kindness and of love. Nor less, I trust,
To them I may have owed another gift,
Of aspect more sublime; that blessed mood,
In which the burden of the mystery,
In which the heavy and the weary weight
Of all this unintelligible world,
Is lightened: – that serene and blessed mood,
In which the affections gently lead us on, –
Until, the breath of this corporeal frame
And even the motion of our human blood
Almost suspended, we are laid asleep
In body, and become a living soul:
While with an eye made quiet by the power
Of harmony, and the deep power of joy,
We see into the life of things.
                                     If this
Be but a vain belief, yet, oh! how oft –
In darkness and amid the many shapes
Of joyless daylight; when the fretful stir
Unprofitable, and the fever of the world,
Have hung upon the beatings of my heart –
How oft, in spirit, have I turned to thee,
O sylvan Wye! thou wanderer through the woods,
How often has my spirit turned to thee!

And now, with gleams of half-extinguished thought,
With many recognitions dim and faint,
And somewhat of a sad perplexity,
The picture of the mind revives again:
While here I stand, not only with the sense
Of present pleasure, but with pleasing thoughts
That in this moment there is life and food
For future years. And so I dare to hope,
Though changed, no doubt, from what I was when first
I came among these hills; when like a roe
I bounded o'er the mountains, by the sides
Of the deep rivers, and the lonely streams,
Wherever nature led: more like a man
Flying from something that he dreads, than one
Who sought the thing he loved. For nature then
(The coarser pleasures of my boyish days,
And their glad animal movements all gone by)
To me was all in all. – I cannot paint
What then I was. The sounding cataract
Haunted me like a passion: the tall rock,
The mountain, and the deep and gloomy wood,
Their colours and their forms, were then to me
An appetite; a feeling and a love,
That had no need of a remoter charm,
By thought supplied, nor any interest
Unborrowed from the eye. – That time is past,
And all its aching joys are now no more,
And all its dizzy raptures. Not for this
Faint I, nor mourn nor murmur; other gifts
Have followed; for such loss, I would believe,
Abundant recompense. For I have learned
To look on nature, not as in the hour
Of thoughtless youth; but hearing oftentimes
The still, sad music of humanity,
Nor harsh nor grating, though of ample power
To chasten and subdue. And I have felt
A presence that disturbs me with the joy
Of elevated thoughts; a sense sublime
Of something far more deeply interfused,

Whose dwelling is the light of setting suns,
And the round ocean and the living air,
And the blue sky, and in the mind of man:
A motion and a spirit, that impels
All thinking things, all objects of all thought,
And rolls through all things. Therefore am I still
A lover of the meadows and the woods,
And mountains; and of all that we behold
From this green earth; of all the mighty world
Of eye, and ear, – both what they half create,
And what perceive; well pleased to recognize
In nature and the language of the sense,
The anchor of my purest thoughts, the nurse,
The guide, the guardian of my heart, and soul
Of all my moral being.
                    Nor perchance,
If I were not thus taught, should I the more
Suffer my genial spirits to decay:
For thou art with me here upon the banks
Of this fair river; thou my dearest Friend,
My dear, dear Friend; and in thy voice I catch
The language of my former heart, and read
My former pleasures in the shooting lights
Of thy wild eyes. Oh! yet a little while
May I behold in thee what I was once,
My dear, dear Sister! and this prayer I make,
Knowing that Nature never did betray
The heart that loved her; 'tis her privilege,
Through all the years of this our life, to lead
From joy to joy: for she can so inform
The mind that is within us, so impress
With quietness and beauty, and so feed
With lofty thoughts, that neither evil tongues,
Rash judgements, nor the sneers of selfish men,
Nor greetings where no kindness is, nor all
The dreary intercourse of daily life,
Shall e'er prevail against us, or disturb
Our cheerful faith, that all which we behold
Is full of blessings. Therefore let the moon

Shine on thee in thy solitary walk;
And let the misty mountain-winds be free
To blow against thee: and, in after years,
When these wild ecstasies shall be matured
Into a sober pleasure; when thy mind
Shall be a mansion for all lovely forms,
Thy memory be as a dwelling-place
For all sweet sounds and harmonies; oh! then,
If solitude, or fear, or pain, or grief,
Should be thy portion, with what healing thoughts
Of tender joy wilt thou remember me,
And these my exhortations! Nor, perchance –
If I should be where I no more can hear
Thy voice, nor catch from thy wild eyes these gleams
Of past existence – wilt thou then forget
That on the banks of this delightful stream
We stood together; and that I, so long
A worshipper of Nature, hither came
Unwearied in that service: rather say
With warmer love – oh! with far deeper zeal
Of holier love. Nor wilt thou then forget,
That after many wanderings, many years
Of absence, these steep woods and lofty cliffs,
And this green pastoral landscape, were to me
More dear, both for themselves and for thy sake!

WILLIAM WORDSWORTH

'Bright star! would I were steadfast as thou art'

Bright star! would I were steadfast as thou art –
    Not in lone splendour hung aloft the night
And watching, with eternal lids apart,
    Like nature's patient, sleepless Eremite,
The moving waters at their priestlike task
    Of pure ablution round earth's human shores,
Or gazing on the new soft-fallen mask
    Of snow upon the mountains and the moors –

71

No – yet still steadfast, still unchangeable,
   Pillowed upon my fair love's ripening breast,
To feel for ever its soft swell and fall,
   Awake for ever in a sweet unrest,
Still, still to hear her tender-taken breath,
And so live ever – or else swoon to death.

JOHN KEATS

To Autumn

Season of mists and mellow fruitfulness,
   Close bosom-friend of the maturing sun,
Conspiring with him how to load and bless
   With fruit the vines that round the thatch-eves run;
To bend with apples the mossed cottage-trees,
   And fill all fruit with ripeness to the core;
     To swell the gourd, and plump the hazel shells
   With a sweet kernel; to set budding more,
And still more, later flowers for the bees,
Until they think warm days will never cease,
     For summer has o'er-brimmed their clammy cells.

Who hath not seen thee oft amid thy store?
   Sometimes whoever seeks abroad may find
Thee sitting careless on a granary floor,
   Thy hair soft-lifted by the winnowing wind;
Or on a half-reaped furrow sound asleep,
   Drowsed with the fume of poppies, while thy hook
     Spares the next swath and all its twinèd flowers;
And sometimes like a gleaner thou dost keep
   Steady thy laden head across a brook;
   Or by a cider-press, with patient look,
     Thou watchest the last oozings hours by hours.

Where are the songs of Spring? Ay, where are they?
   Think not of them, thou hast thy music too –
While barrèd clouds bloom the soft-dying day,
   And touch the stubble-plains with rosy hue:
Then in a wailful choir the small gnats mourn

Among the river sallows, borne aloft
  Or sinking as the light wind lives or dies;
And full-grown lambs loud bleat from hilly bourn;
  Hedge-crickets sing; and now with treble soft
  The red-breast whistles from a garden-croft;
    And gathering swallows twitter in the skies.

JOHN KEATS

Rondeau

Jenny kissed me when we met,
  Jumping from the chair she sat in;
Time, you thief, who love to get
  Sweets into your list, put that in!
Say I'm weary, say I'm sad,
  Say that health and wealth have missed me,
Say I'm growing old, but add,
  Jenny kissed me.

JAMES LEIGH HUNT

A Sonnet

Lift not the painted veil which those who live
Call Life: though unreal shapes be pictured there,
And it but mimic all we would believe
With colours idly spread, – behind, lurk Fear
And Hope, twin Destinies; who ever weave
Their shadows, o'er the chasm, sightless and drear.
I knew one who had lifted it – he sought,
For his lost heart was tender, things to love,
But found them not, alas! nor was there aught
The world contains, the which he could approve.
Through the unheeding many he did move,
A splendour among shadows, a bright blot
Upon this gloomy scene, a Spirit that strove
For truth, and like the Preacher found it not.

PERCY BYSSHE SHELLEY

Hesperus

Hesperus, the day is gone
Soft falls the silent dew
A tear is now on many a flower
And heaven lives in you.

Hesperus, the evening mild
Falls round us soft and sweet;
'Tis like the breathings of a child
When day and evening meet.

Hesperus, the closing flower
Sleeps on the dewy ground,
While dews fall in a silent shower
And heaven breathes around

Hesperus, thy twinkling ray
Beams in the blue of heaven
And tells the traveller on his way
That earth shall be forgiven.

JOHN CLARE

Ode on a Grecian Urn

Thou still unravished bride of quietness,
    Thou foster-child of silence and slow time,
Sylvan historian, who canst thus express
    A flowery tale more sweetly than our rhyme:
What leaf-fringed legend haunts about thy shape
    Of deities or mortals, or of both,
        In Tempe or the dales of Arcady?
    What men or gods are these? What maidens loth?
What mad pursuit? What struggle to escape?
        What pipes and timbrels? What wild ecstasy?

Heard melodies are sweet, but those unheard
    Are sweeter; therefore, ye soft pipes, play on;

Not to the sensual ear, but, more endeared,
    Pipe to the spirit ditties of no tone:
Fair youth, beneath the trees, thou canst not leave
    Thy song, nor ever can those trees be bare;
        Bold Lover, never, never canst thou kiss,
Though winning near the goal – yet, do not grieve:
    She cannot fade, though thou hast not thy bliss,
        For ever wilt thou love, and she be fair!

Ah, happy, happy boughs! that cannot shed
    Your leaves, nor ever bid the Spring adieu;
And, happy melodist, unwearièd,
    For ever piping songs for ever new;
More happy love! more happy, happy love!
    For ever warm and still to be enjoyed,
        For ever panting, and for ever young –
All breathing human passion far above,
    That leaves a heart high-sorrowful and cloyed,
        A burning forehead, and a parching tongue.

Who are these coming to the sacrifice?
    To what green altar, O mysterious priest,
Lead'st thou that heifer lowing at the skies,
    And all her silken flanks with garlands dressed?
What little town by river or sea shore,
    Or mountain-built with peaceful citadel,
        Is emptied of this folk, this pious morn?
And, little town, thy streets for evermore
    Will silent be; and not a soul to tell
        Why thou art desolate, can e'er return.

O Attic shape! Fair attitude! with brede
    Of marble men and maidens overwrought,
With forest branches and the trodden weed;
    Thou, silent form, dost tease us out of thought
As doth eternity: Cold Pastoral!
    When old age shall this generation waste,
        Thou shalt remain, in midst of other woe
            Than ours, a friend to man, to whom thou say'st,

'Beauty is truth, truth beauty, – that is all
Ye know on earth, and all ye need to know.'

JOHN KEATS

'This living hand, now warm and capable'

This living hand, now warm and capable
Of earnest grasping, would, if it were cold
And in the icy silence of the tomb,
So haunt thy days and chill thy dreaming nights
That thou would wish thine own heart dry of blood
So in my veins red life might stream again,
And thou be conscience-calmed – see here it is –
I hold it towards you.

JOHN KEATS

'I am'

I am – yet what I am, none cares or knows;
   My friends forsake me like a memory lost:
I am the self-consumer of my woes –
   They rise and vanish in oblivion's host
Like shadows in love-frenzied stifled throes
   And yet I am, and live – like vapours tost

Into the nothingness of scorn and noise,
   Into the living sea of waking dreams,
Where there is neither sense of life or joys,
   But the vast shipwreck of my life's esteems;
Even the dearest that I love the best
   Are strange – nay, rather, stranger than the rest.

I long for scenes where man hath never trod
   A place where woman never smiled or wept
There to abide with my Creator, God,
   And sleep as I in childhood sweetly slept,
Untroubling and untroubled where I lie
   The grass below – above, the vaulted sky.

JOHN CLARE

'After dark vapours have oppressed our plains'

After dark vapours have oppressed our plains
   For a long dreary season, comes a day
   Born of the gentle South, and clears away
From the sick heavens all unseemly stains.
The anxious moth, relieving from its pains,
   Takes as a long-lost right the feel of May,
   The eyelids with the passing coolness play,
Like rose leaves with the drip of summer rains.
And calmest thoughts come round us – as of leaves
   Budding – fruit ripening in stillness – autumn suns
Smiling at eve upon the quiet sheaves –
Sweet Sappho's cheek – a sleeping infant's breath –
   The gradual sand that through an hour-glass runs –
A woodland rivulet – a Poet's death.

JOHN KEATS

To Sleep

O soft embalmer of the still midnight,
   Shutting, with careful fingers and benign,
Our gloom-pleased eyes, embowered from the light,
   Enshaded in forgetfulness divine:
O soothest Sleep! if so it please thee, close
   In midst of this thine hymn, my willing eyes,
Or wait the 'Amen', ere the poppy throws
   Around my bed its lulling charities.
Then save me, or the passèd day will shine
Upon my pillow, breeding many woes;
   Save me from curious conscience, that still hoards
Its strength for darkness, burrowing like the mole;
   Turn the key deftly in the oilèd wards,
And seal the hushèd casket of my soul.

JOHN KEATS

The Yellowhammer

When shall I see the white thorn leaves agen
And Yellowhammers gath'ring the dry bents
By the Dyke side on stilly moor or fen
Feathered wi love and natures good intents?
Rude is the nest this Architect invents,
Rural the place wi cart ruts by dyke side
Dead grass, horse hair and downy headed bents
Tied to dead thistles she doth well provide,
Close to a hill o' ants where cowslips bloom
And shed o'er meadows far their sweet perfume.
In early Spring when winds blow chilly cold
The yellow hammer trailing grass will come
To fix a place and choose an early home
With yellow breast and head of solid gold.

JOHN CLARE

Winter Evening

The crib-stock fothered horses suppered-up
And cows in sheds all littered-down in straw
The threshers gone, the owls are left to whoop
The ducks go waddling with distended craw
Through little hole made in the henroost door
And geese with idle gabble never o'er
Bate careless hog untill he tumbles down
Insult provoking spite to noise the more
While fowl high-perched blink with contemptuous frown
On all the noise and bother heard below
Over the stable ridge in crowds the crow
With jackdaws intermixed known by their noise
To the warm woods behind the village go
And whistling home for bed go weary boys.

JOHN CLARE

First Sight of Spring

The hazel blooms, in threads of crimson hue,
Peep through the swelling buds and look for spring
Ere yet a whitethorn leaf appears in view
Or March finds throstles pleased enough to sing
On the old touchwood tree woodpeckers cling
A moment and their harsh-toned notes renew.
In happier mood the stockdove claps his wing
The squirrel sputters up the powdered oak
With tail cocked o'er his head and ears erect
Startled to hear the woodman's understroke
And with the courage that his fears collect
He hisses fierce, half malice and half glee,
Leaping from branch to branch about the tree
In winter's foliage moss and lichens drest.

JOHN CLARE

Snow Storm

What a night the wind howls hisses and but stops
To howl more loud while the snow volly keeps
Insessant batter at the window pane
Making our comfort feel as sweet again
And in the morning when the tempest drops
At every cottage-door mountainious heaps
Of snow lies drifted that all entrance stops
Untill the beesom and the shovel gains
The path – and leaves a wall on either side –
The shepherd rambling valleys white and wide
With new sensations his old memorys fills
When hedges left at night, no more descried
Are turned to one white sweep of curving hills
And trees, turned bushes, half their bodys hide.

The boy that goes to fodder with supprise
Walks o'er the gate he opened yesternight
The hedges all have vanished from his eyes

E'en some tree tops the sheep could reach to bite
The novel scene emboldens new delight
And though with cautious steps his sports begin
He bolder shuffles the huge hills of snow
Till down he drops and plunges to the chin
And struggles much and oft escape to win
Then turns and laughs but dare not further go
For deep the grass and bushes lie below
Where little birds that soon at eve went in
With heads tucked in their wings now pine for day
And little feel boys o'er their heads can stray.

JOHN CLARE

Night Wind

Darkness like midnight from the sobbing woods
Clamours with dismal tidings of the rain
Roaring as rivers breaking loose in floods
To spread and foam and deluge all the plain
The cotter listens at his door again
Half doubting whether it be floods or wind
And through the thickening darkness looks affraid
Thinking of roads that travel has to find
Through night's black depths in danger's garb arrayed
And the loud glabber round the flaze soon stops
When hushed to silence by the lifted hand
Of fearing dame who hears the noise in dread
And thinks a deluge comes to drown the land
Nor dares she go to bed untill the tempest drops.

JOHN CLARE

Evening Schoolboys

Harken that happy shout – the school-house door
Is open thrown and out the younkers' teem
Some run to leapfrog on the rushy moor
And others dabble in the shallow stream

Catching young fish and turning pebbles o'er
For mussel clams – Look in that mellow gleam
Where the retiring sun that rests the while
Streams through the broken hedge. – How happy seem
Those schoolboy friendships leaning o'er the stile
Both reading in one book – anon a dream
Rich with new joys doth their young hearts beguile
And the book's pocketed most hastily
Ah happy boys well may ye turn and smile
When joys are yours that never cost a sigh.

JOHN CLARE

Composed Upon Westminster Bridge,
September 3, 1802

Earth has not anything to show more fair:
Dull would he be of soul who could pass by
A sight so touching in its majesty:
This City now doth, like a garment, wear
The beauty of the morning; silent, bare,
Ships, towers, domes, theatres, and temples lie
Open unto the fields, and to the sky;
All bright and glittering in the smokeless air.
Never did sun more beautifully steep
In his first splendour, valley, rock, or hill;
Ne'er saw I, never felt, a calm so deep!
The river glideth at his own sweet will:
Dear God! the very houses seem asleep;
And all that mighty heart is lying still!

WILLIAM WORDSWORTH

'I wandered lonely as a cloud'

I wandered lonely as a cloud
That floats on high o'er vales and hills,
When all at once I saw a crowd,
A host, of golden daffodils;

Beside the lake, beneath the trees,
Fluttering and dancing in the breeze.

Continuous as the stars that shine
And twinkle on the milky way,
They stretched in never-ending line
Along the margin of the bay:
Ten thousnd saw I at a glance,
Tossing their heads in sprightly dance.

The waves beside them danced; but they
Out-did the sparkling waves in glee:
A poet could not but be gay,
In such a jocund company:
I gazed – and gazed – but little thought
What wealth the show to me had brought:

For oft, when on my couch I lie
In vacant or in pensive mood,
They flash upon that inward eye
Which is the bliss of solitude;
And then my heart with pleasure fills,
And dances with the daffodils.

WILLIAM WORDSWORTH

The Badger

The badger grunting on his woodland track
With shaggy hide and sharp nose scrowed with black
Roots in the bushes and the woods and makes
A great huge burrow in the ferns and brakes
With nose on ground he runs an awkard pace
And anything will beat him in the race
The shepherd's dog will run him to his den
Followed and hooted by the dogs and men
The woodman when the hunting comes about
Go round at night to stop the foxes out
And hurrying through the bushes ferns and brakes
Nor sees the many holes the badger makes

And often through the bushes to the chin
Breaks the old holes and tumbles headlong in.

Some keep a baited badger tame as hog
And tame him till he follows like the dog
They urge him on like dogs and show fair play
He beats and scarcely wounded goes away
Lapt up as if asleep he scorns to fly
And siezes any dog that ventures nigh
Clapt like a dog he never bites the men
But worrys dogs and hurrys to his den
They let him out and turn a harrow down
And there he fights the host of all the town
He licks the patting hand and trys to play
And never trys to bite or run away
And runs away from noise in hollow trees
Burnt by the boys to get a swarm of bees.
When midnight comes a host of dogs and men

Go out and track the badger to his den
And put a sack within the hole and lye
Till the old grunting badger passes bye
He comes and hears they let the strongest loose
The old fox hears the noise and drops the goose
The poacher shoots and hurrys from the cry
And the old hare half-wounded buzzes bye
They get a forked stick to bear him down
And clap the dogs and bear him to the town
And bait him all the day with many dogs
And laugh and shout and fright the scampering hogs
He runs along and bites at all he meets
They shout and hollo down the noisey streets.

He turns about to face the loud uproar
And drives the rebels to their very doors
The frequent stone is hurled where e'er they go
When badgers fight and every one's a foe
The dogs are clapt and urged to join the fray
The badger turns and drives them all away
Though scarcly half as big, dimute and small,

He fights with dogs for hours and beats them all
The heavy mastiff savage in the fray
Lies down and licks his feet and turns away
The bull-dog knows his match and waxes cold
The badger grins and never leaves his hold
He drives the crowd and follows at their heels
And bites them through. The drunkard swears and reels,

The frighted women takes the boys away
The blackguard laughs and hurrys on the fray:
He tries to reach the woods, an awkard race,
But sticks and cudgels quickly stop the chace
He turns agen and drives the noisey crowd
And beats the many dogs in noises loud
He drives away and beats them every one
And then they loose them all and set them on
He falls as dead and kicked by boys and men
Then starts and grins and drives the crowd agen
Till kicked and torn and beaten out he lies
And leaves his hold and cackles groans and dies.

JOHN CLARE

On the Grasshopper and Cricket

The poetry of earth is never dead:
   When all the birds are faint with the hot sun,
    And hide in cooling trees, a voice will run
From hedge to hedge about the new-mown mead –
That is the Grasshopper's. He takes the lead
   In summer luxury; he has never done
    With his delights, for when tired out with fun
He rests at ease beneath some pleasant weed.
The poetry of earth is ceasing never:
   On a lone winter evening, when the frost
    Has wrought a silence, from the stove there shrills
The Cricket's song, in warmth increasing ever,
   And seems to one in drowsiness half lost,
    The Grasshopper's among some grassy hills.

JOHN KEATS

'Over the hill and over the dale'

Over the hill and over the dale,
And over the bourn to Dawlish –
Where gingerbread wives have a scanty sale
And gingerbread nuts are smallish.

Rantipole Betty she ran down a hill
And kicked up her petticoats fairly.
Says I, 'I'll be Jack if you will be Jill.'
So she sat on the grass debonairly.

'Here's somebody coming, here's somebody coming!'
Says I, ''Tis the wind at a parley.'
So without any fuss, any hawing and humming,
She lay on the grass debonairly.

'Here's somebody here, and here's somebody *there*!'
Says I, 'Hold your tongue, you young gipsy.'
So she held her tongue and lay plump and fair,
And dead as a Venus tipsy.

O who wouldn't hie to Dawlish fair,
O who wouldn't stop in a meadow?
O [who] would not rumple the daisies there,
And make the wild fern for a bed do?

JOHN KEATS

'Old Meg she was a gipsy'

Old Meg she was a gipsy,
    And lived upon the moors,
Her bed it was the brown heath turf,
    And her house was out of doors.

Her apples were swart blackberries,
    Her currants pods o' broom,
Her wine was dew o' the wild white rose,
    Her book a churchyard tomb.

Her brothers were the craggy hills,
   Her sisters larchen trees –
Alone with her great family
   She lived as she did please.

No breakfast had she many a morn,
   No dinner many a noon,
And 'stead of supper she would stare
   Full hard against the moon.

But every morn of woodbine fresh
   She made her garlanding,
And every night the dark glen yew
   She wove, and she would sing.

And with her fingers old and brown
   She plaited mats o' rushes,
And gave them to the cottagers
   She met among the bushes.

Old Meg was brave as Margaret Queen
   And tall as Amazon,
An old red blanket cloak she wore,
   A chip-hat had she on.
God rest her agèd bones somewhere –
   She died full long agone!

JOHN KEATS

Nutting

It seems a day
(I speak of one from many singled out)
One of those heavenly days that cannot die;
When, in the eagerness of boyish hope,
I left our cottage-threshold, sallying forth
With a huge wallet o'er my shoulders slung,
A nutting-crook in hand; and turned my steps
Toward some far-distant wood, a Figure quaint,
Tricked out in proud disguise of cast-off weeds

86

Which for that service had been husbanded,
By exhortation of my frugal Dame –
Motley accoutrement, of power to smile
At thorns, and brakes, and brambles, – and, in truth,
More ragged than need was! O'er pathless rocks,
Through beds of matted fern, and tangled thickets,
Forcing my way, I came to one dear nook
Unvisited, where not a broken bough
Drooped with its withered leaves, ungracious sign
Of devastation; but the hazels rose
Tall and erect, with tempting clusters hung,
A virgin scene! – A little while I stood,
Breathing with such suppression of the heart
As joy delights in; and, with wise restraint
Voluptuous, fearless of a rival, eyed
The banquet; – or beneath the trees I sate
Among the flowers, and with the flowers I played;
A temper known to those who, after long
And weary expectation, have been blest
With sudden happiness beyond all hope.
Perhaps it was a bower beneath whose leaves
The violets of five seasons re-appear
And fade, unseen by any human eye;
Where fairy water-breaks do murmur on
For ever; and I saw the sparkling foam,
And – with my cheek on one of those green stones
That, fleeced with moss, under the shady trees
Lay round me, scattered like a flock of sheep –
I heard the murmur and the murmuring sound,
In that sweet mood when pleasure loves to pay
Tribute to ease; and, of its joy secure,
The heart luxuriates with indifferent things,
Wasting its kindliness on stocks and stones,
And on the vacant air. Then up I rose,
And dragged to earth both branch and bough, with crash
And merciless ravage: and the shady nook
Of hazels, and the green and mossy bower,
Deformed and sullied, patiently gave up
Their quiet being: and, unless I now

Confound my present feelings with the past,
Ere from the multilated bower I turned
Exulting, rich beyond the wealth of kings,
I felt a sense of pain when I beheld
The silent trees, and saw the intruding sky. –
Then, dearest Maiden, move along these shades
In gentleness of heart; with gentle hand
Touch – for there is a spirit in the woods.

WILLIAM WORDSWORTH

Autumn

The thistledown's flying, though the winds are all still
On the green grass now lying, now mounting the hill.
The spring from the fountain now boils like a pot
Through stones past the counting it bubbles red-hot.

The ground parched and cracked is like overbaked bread,
The greensward all wrecked is bents dried up and dead.
The fallow fields glitter like water indeed,
And gossamers twitter flung from weed unto weed.

Hill-tops like hot iron glitter hot i' the sun,
And the rivers we're eyeing burn to gold as they run.
Burning hot is the ground, liquid gold is the air:
Whoever looks round sees Eternity there.

JOHN CLARE

Haymaking

'Tis haytime and the red-complexioned sun
Was scarcely up ere blackbirds had begun
Along the meadow hedges here and there
To sing loud songs to the sweet-smelling air
Where breath of flowers and grass and happy cow

Fling o'er one's senses streams of fragrance now
While in some pleasant nook the swain and maid
Lean o'er their rakes and loiter in the shade
Or bend a minute o'er the bridge and throw
Crumbs in their leisure to the fish below
– Hark at that happy shout – and song between
'Tis pleasure's birthday in her meadow scene.
What joy seems half so rich from pleasure won
As the loud laugh of maidens in the sun?

JOHN CLARE

Old Man Travelling

  The little hedgerow birds,
That peck along the road, regard him not.
He travels on, and in his face, his step,
His gait, is one expression: every limb,
His look and bending figure, all bespeak
A man who does not move with pain, but moves
With thought. – He is insensibly subdued
To settled quiet: he is one by whom
All effort seems forgotten; one to whom
Long patience hath such mild composure given,
That patience now doth seem a thing of which
He hath no need. He is by nature led
To peace so perfect that the young behold
With envy, what the Old Man hardly feels.
I asked him whither he was bound and what
The object of his journey. He replied:
'Sir, I am going many miles to take
A last leave of my son, a mariner,
Who from a sea fight has been brought to Falmouth
And there is dying in an hospital.

WILLIAM WORDSWORTH

London, 1802

Milton! thou shouldst be living at this hour:
England hath need of thee: she is a fen
Of stagnant waters: altar, sword, and pen,
Fireside, the heroic wealth of hall and bower,
Have forfeited their ancient English dower
Of inward happiness. We are selfish men;
Oh! raise us up, return to us again;
And give us manners, virtue, freedom, power.
Thy soul was like a Star, and dwelt apart:
Thou hadst a voice whose sound was like the sea:
Pure as the naked heavens, majestic, free,
So didst thou travel on life's common way,
In cheerful godliness; and yet thy heart
The lowliest duties on herself did lay.

WILLIAM WORDSWORTH

Autumn Morning

The autumn morning waked by many a gun
Throws o'er the fields her many-coloured light
Wood wildly touched close-tanned and stubbles dun
A motley paradise for earth's delight
Clouds ripple as the darkness breaks to light
And clover fields are hid with silver mist
One shower of cobwebs o'er the surface spread
And threads of silk in strange disorder twist
Round every leaf and blossom's bottly head.
Hares in the drowning herbage scarcely steal
But on the battered pathway squats abed
And by the cart-rut nips her morning meal
Look where we may the scene is strange and new
And every object wears a changing hue.

JOHN CLARE

The Small Celandine

There is a Flower, the lesser Celandine,
That shrinks, like many more, from cold and rain;
And, the first moment that the sun may shine,
Bright as the sun himself, 'tis out again!

When hailstones have been falling, swarm on swarm,
Or blasts the green field and the trees distrest,
Oft have I seen it muffled up from harm,
In close self-shelter, like a Thing at rest.

But lately, one rough day, this Flower I passed
And recognized it, though an altered form,
Now standing forth an offering to the blast,
And buffeted at will by rain and storm.

I stopped, and said with inly-muttered voice,
'It doth not love the shower, nor seek the cold:
This neither is its courage nor its choice,
But its necessity in being old.

'The sunshine may not cheer it, nor the dew;
It cannot help itself in its decay;
Stiff in its members, withered, changed of hue.'
And, in my spleen, I smiled that it was grey.

To be a Prodigal's Favourite – then, worse truth,
A Miser's Pensioner – behold our lot!
O Man, that from thy fair and shining youth
Age might but take the things Youth needed not!

WILLIAM WORDSWORTH

Evening

'Tis evening, the black snail has got on his track,
And gone to its nest is the wren; –
And the packman snail too, with his home on his back;
Clings on the bowed bents like a wen.

The shepherd has made a rude mark with his foot,
Where his shadow reached when he first came;
And it just touched the tree where his secret love cut,
Two letters that stand for love's name.

The evening comes in with the wishes of love; –
And the shepherd he looks on the flowers; –
And thinks who would praise the soft song of the dove,
And meet joy in these dewfalling hours.

For nature is love, and the wishers of love;
When nothing can hear or intrude;
It hides from the eagle, and joins with the dove:
In beautiful green solitude.

JOHN CLARE

The Mermaidens' Vesper-hymn

Troop home to silent grots and caves!
Troop home! and mimic as you go
The mournful winding of the waves
Which to their dark abysses flow!

At this sweet hour, all things beside
In amorous pairs to covert creep;
The swans that brush the evening tide
Homeward in snowy couples keep;

In his green den the murmuring seal
Close by his sleek companion lies;
While singly we to bedward steal,
And close in fruitless sleep our eyes.

In bowers of love men take their rest,
In loveless bowers we sigh alone!
With bosom-friends are others blest, –
But we have none! But we have none!

GEORGE DARLEY

Eternity

He who binds to himself a joy
Does the winged life destroy;
But he who kisses the joy as it flies
Lives in eternity's sunrise.

WILLIAM BLAKE

'Surprised by joy'

Surprised by joy – impatient as the Wind
I turned to share the transport – Oh! with whom
But Thee, deep buried in the silent tomb,
That spot which no vicissitude can find?
Love, faithful love, recalled thee to my mind –
But how could I forget thee? Through what power,
Even for the least division of an hour,
Have I been so beguiled as to be blind
To my most grievous loss – That thought's return
Was the worst pang that sorrow ever bore,
Save one, one only, when I stood forlorn,
Knowing my heart's best treasure was no more;
That neither present time, nor years unborn
Could to my sight that heavenly face restore.

WILLIAM WORDSWORTH

The Rime of the Ancient Mariner

PART I

It is an ancient Mariner,
And he stoppeth one of three.
'By thy long grey beard and glittering eye,
Now wherefore stopp'st thou me?

'The Bridegroom's doors are opened wide,
And I am next of kin;
The guests are met, the feast is set:
May'st hear the merry din.'

93

He holds him with his skinny hand,
'There was a ship,' quoth he.
'Hold off! unhand me, grey-bearded loon!'
Eftsoons his hand dropt he.

He holds him with his glittering eye –
The Wedding-Guest stood still,
And listens like a three years' child:
The Mariner hath his will.

The Wedding-Guest sat on a stone:
He cannot choose but hear;
And thus spake on that ancient man,
The bright-eyed Mariner.

The ship was cheered, the harbour cleared,
Merrily did we drop
Below the kirk, below the hill,
Below the light house top.

The Sun came up upon the left,
Out of the sea came he!
And he shone bright, and on the right
Went down into the sea.

Higher and higher every day,
Till over the mast at noon –
The Wedding-Guest here beat his breast,
For he heard the loud bassoon.

The bride hath paced into the hall,
Red as a rose is she;
Nodding their heads before her goes
The merry minstrelsy.

The Wedding-Guest he beat his breast,
Yet he cannot choose but hear;
And thus spake on that ancient man,
The bright-eyed Mariner.

And now the Storm-blast came, and he
Was tyrannous and strong:

He struck with his o'ertaking wings,
And chased us south along.

With sloping masts and dipping prow,
As who pursued with yell and blow
Still treads the shadow of his foe,
And forward bends his head,
The ship drove fast, loud roared the blast,
And southward aye we fled.

And now there came both mist and snow,
And it grew wondrous cold:
And ice, mast-high, came floating by,
As green as emerald.

And through the drifts the snowy clifts
Did send a dismal sheen:
Nor shapes of men nor beasts we ken –
The ice was all between.

The ice was here, the ice was there,
The ice was all around:
It cracked and growled, and roared and howled
Like noises in a swound!

At length did cross an Albatross,
Thorough the fog it came;
As if it had been a Christian soul,
We hailed it in God's name.

It ate the food it ne'er had eat,
And round and round it flew.
The ice did split with a thunder-fit;
The helmsman steered us through!

And a good south wind sprung up behind;
The Albatross did follow,
And every day, for food or play,
Came to the mariners' hollo!

In mist or cloud, on mast or shroud,
It perched for vespers nine;

Whiles all the night, through fog-smoke white,
Glimmered the white moon-shine.

'God save thee, ancient Mariner!
From the fiends, that plague thee thus! –
Why look'st thou so? – With my cross-bow
I shot the Albatross.

PART II

The sun now rose upon the right:
Out of the sea came he,
Still hid in mist, and on the left
Went down into the sea.

And the good south wind still blew behind,
But no sweet bird did follow,
Nor any day for food or play
Came to the mariners' hollo!

And I had done a hellish thing,
And it would work 'em woe:
For all averred, I had killed the bird
That made the breeze to blow
Ah wretch! said they, the bird to slay,
That made the breeze to blow!

Nor dim nor red, like God's own head,
The glorious Sun uprist:
Then all averred, I had killed the bird
That brought the fog and mist.
'Twas right, said they, such birds to slay,
That bring the fog and mist.

The fair breeze blew, the white foam flew,
The furrow followed free;
We were the first that ever burst
Into that silent sea.

Down dropt the breeze, the sails dropt down,
'Twas sad as sad could be;
And we did speak only to break
The silence of the sea!

All in a hot and copper sky,
The bloody Sun, at noon,
Right up above the mast did stand,
No bigger than the Moon.

Day after day, day after day,
We stuck, nor breath nor motion;
As idle as a painted ship
Upon a painted ocean.

Water, water, every where,
And all the boards did shrink;
Water, water, every where,
Nor any drop to drink.

The very deep did rot: O Christ!
That ever this should be!
Yea, slimy things did crawl with legs
Upon the slimy sea.

About, about, in reel and rout
The death-fires danced at night;
The water, like a witch's oils,
Burnt green, and blue and white.

And some in dreams assured were
Of the spirit that plagued us so;
Nine fathom deep he had followed us
From the land of mist and snow.

And every tongue, through utter drought,
Was withered at the root;
We could not speak, no more than if
We had been choked with soot.

Ah! well a-day! what evil looks
Had I from old and young!
Instead of the cross, the Albatross
About my neck was hung.

PART III

There passed a weary time. Each throat
Was parched, and glazed each eye.
A weary time! a weary time!
How glazed each weary eye,
When looking westward, I beheld
A something in the sky.

At first it seemed a little speck,
And then it seemed a mist;
It moved and moved, and took at last
A certain shape, I wist.

A speck, a mist, a shape, I wist!
And still it neared and neared:
As if it dodged a water-sprite,
It plunged and tacked and veered.

With throats unslaked, with black lips baked,
We could nor laugh nor wail;
Through utter drought all dumb we stood!
I bit my arm, I sucked the blood,
And cried, A sail! a sail!

With throats unslaked, with black lips baked,
Agape they heard me call:
Gramercy! they for joy did grin,
And all at once their breath drew in,
As they were drinking all.

See! see! (I cried) she tacks no more!
Hither to work us weal;
Without a breeze, without a tide,
She steadies with upright keel!

The western wave was all a-flame.
The day was well nigh done!
Almost upon the western wave
Rested the broad bright Sun;
When that strange shape drove suddenly
Betwixt us and the Sun.

And straight the Sun was flecked with bars,
(Heaven's Mother send us grace!)
As if through a dungeon-grate he peered
With broad and burning face.

Alas! (thought I, and my heart beat loud)
How fast she nears and nears!
Are those her sails that glance in the Sun,
Like restless gossameres?

Are those her ribs through which the Sun
Did peer, as through a grate?
And is that Woman all her crew?
Is that a Death? and are there two?
Is Death that woman's mate?

Her lips were red, her looks were free,
Her locks were yellow as gold:
Her skin was as white as leprosy,
The Night-mare Life-in-Death was she,
Who thicks man's blood with cold.

The naked hulk alongside came,
And the twain were casting dice;
'The game is done! I've won, I've won!'
Quoth she, and whistles thrice.

The Sun's rim dips; the stars rush out:
At one stride comes the dark;
With far-heard whisper, o'er the sea,
Off shot the spectre-bark.

We listened and looked sideways up!
Fear at my heart, as at a cup,
My life-blood seemed to sip!
The stars were dim, and thick the night,
The steersman's face by his lamp gleamed white;
From the sails the dew did drip –
Till clomb above the eastern bar
The hornèd Moon, with one bright star
Within the nether tip.

One after one, by the star-dogged Moon,
Too quick for groan or sigh,
Each turned his face with a ghastly pang,
And cursed me with his eye.

Four times fifty living men,
(And I heard nor sigh nor groan)
With heavy thump, a lifeless lump,
They dropped down one by one.

The souls did from their bodies fly, –
They fled to bliss or woe!
And every soul, it passed me by,
Like the whizz of my cross-bow!

PART IV

'I fear thee, ancient Mariner!
I fear thy skinny hand!
And thou art long, and lank, and brown,
As is the ribbed sea-sand.

I fear thee and thy glittering eye,
And thy skinny hand, so brown.' –
Fear not, fear not, thou Wedding-Guest!
This body dropt not down.

Alone, alone, all, all alone,
Alone on a wide wide sea!
And never a saint took pity on
My soul in agony.

The many men, so beautiful!
And they all dead did lie:
And a thousand thousand slimy things
Lived on; and so did I.

I looked upon the rotting sea,
And drew my eyes away;
I looked upon the rotting deck,
And there the dead men lay.

I looked to heaven, and tried to pray;
But or ever a prayer had gusht,
A wicked whisper came, and made
My heart as dry as dust.

I closed my lids, and kept them close,
And the balls like pulses beat;
For the sky and the sea, and the sea and the sky
Lay like a load on my weary eye,
And the dead were at my feet.

The cold sweat melted from their limbs,
Nor rot nor reek did they:
The look with which they looked on me
Had never passed away.

An orphan's curse would drag to hell
A spirit from on high;
But oh! more horrible than that
Is the curse in a dead man's eye!
Seven days, seven nights, I saw that curse,
And yet I could not die.

The moving Moon went up the sky,
And no where did abide:
Softly she was going up,
And a star or two beside –

Her beams bemocked the sultry main,
Like April hoar-frost spread;
But where the ship's huge shadow lay,
The charmèd water burnt alway
A still and awful red.

Beyond the shadow of the ship,
I watched the water-snakes:
They moved in tracks of shining white,
And when they reared, the elfish light
Fell off in hoary flakes.

Within the shadow of the ship
I watched their rich attire:
Blue, glossy green, and velvet black,

They coiled and swam; and every track
Was a flash of golden fire.

O happy living things! no tongue
Their beauty might declare:
A spring of love gushed from my heart,
And I blessed them unaware:
Sure my kind saint took pity on me,
And I blessed them unaware.

The selfsame moment I could pray:
And from my neck so free
The Albatross fell off, and sank
Like lead into the sea.

PART V

Oh sleep! it is a gentle thing,
Beloved from pole to pole!
To Mary Queen the praise be given!
She sent the gentle sleep from Heaven,
That slid into my soul.

The silly buckets on the deck,
That had so long remained,
I dreamt that they were filled with dew;
And when I awoke, it rained.

My lips were wet, my throat was cold,
My garments all were dank;
Sure I had drunken in my dreams,
And still my body drank.

I moved, and could not feel my limbs:
I was so light – almost
I thought that I had died in sleep,
And was a blessèd ghost.

And soon I heard a roaring wind:
It did not come anear;
But with its sound it shook the sails,
That were so thin and sere.

The upper air burst into life!
And a hundred fire-flags sheen,
To and fro they were hurried about!
And to and fro, and in and out,
The wan stars danced between.

And the coming wind did roar more loud,
And the sails did sigh like sedge;
And the rain poured down from one black cloud;
The Moon was at its edge.

The thick black cloud was cleft, and still
The Moon was at its side:
Like waters shot from some high crag,
The lightning fell with never a jag,
A river steep and wide.

The loud wind never reached the ship,
Yet now the ship moved on!
Beneath the lightning and the moon
The dead men gave a groan.

They groaned, they stirred, they all uprose,
Nor spake, nor moved their eyes;
It had been strange, even in a dream,
To have seen those dead men rise.

The helmsman steered, the ship moved on;
Yet never a breeze up blew;
The mariners all 'gan work the ropes,
Where they were wont to do;
They raised their limbs like lifeless tools –
We were a ghastly crew.

The body of my brother's son
Stood by me, knee to knee:
The body and I pulled at one rope,
But he said nought to me.

'I fear thee, ancient Mariner!'
Be calm, thou Wedding-Guest!
'Twas not those souls that fled in pain,

Which to their corses came again,
But a troop of spirits blest:

For when it dawned – they dropped their arms,
And clustered round the mast;
Sweet sounds rose slowly through their mouths,
And from their bodies passed.

Around, around, flew each sweet sound,
Then darted to the Sun;
Slowly the sounds came back again,
Now mixed, now one by one.

Sometimes a-dropping from the sky
I heard the sky-lark sing;
Sometimes all little birds that are,
How they seemed to fill the sea and air
With their sweet jargoning!

And now 'twas like all instruments,
Now like a lonely flute;
And now it is an angel's song,
That makes the heavens be mute.

It ceased; yet still the sails made on
A pleasant noise till noon,
A noise like of a hidden brook
In the leafy month of June,
That to the sleeping woods all night
Singeth a quiet tune.

Till noon we quietly sailed on,
Yet never a breeze did breathe:
Slowly and smoothly went the ship,
Moved onward from beneath:

Under the keel nine fathom deep,
From the land of mist and snow,
The spirit slid; and it was he
That made the ship to go.
The sails at noon left off their tune,
And the ship stood still also.

The Sun, right up above the mast,
Had fixed her to the ocean:
But in a mintute she 'gan stir,
With a short uneasy motion –
Backwards and forwards half her length
With a short uneasy motion.

Then like a pawing horse let go,
She made a sudden bound:
It flung the blood into my head,
And I fell down in a swound.

How long in that same fit I lay,
I have not to declare;
But ere my living life returned,
I heard, and in my soul discerned
Two voices in the air.

'Is it he?' quoth one, 'Is this the man?
By him who died on cross,
With his cruel bow he laid full low
The harmless Albatross.

'The spirit who bideth by himself
In the land of mist and snow,
He loved the bird that loved the man
Who shot him with his bow.'

The other was a softer voice,
As soft as honey-dew:
Quoth he, 'The man hath penance done,
And penance more will do.'

PART VI

First Voice
But tell me, tell me! speak again,
Thy soft response renewing –
What makes that ship drive on so fast?
What is the ocean doing?

Second Voice

Still as a slave before his lord,
The ocean hath no blast;
His great bright eye most silently
Up to the Moon is cast –

If he may know which way to go;
For she guides him smooth or grim.
See, brother, see! how graciously
She looketh down on him.

First Voice

But why drives on that ship so fast,
Without or wave or wind?

Second Voice

The air is cut away before,
And closes from behind.

Fly, brother, fly! more high, more high!
Or we shall be belated:
For slow and slow that ship will go,
When the Mariner's trance is abated.

I woke, and were sailing on
As in a gentle weather:
'Twas night, calm night, the Moon was high;
The dead men stood together.

All stood together on the deck,
For a charnel-dungeon fitter:
All fixed on me their stony eyes,
That in the Moon did glitter.

The pang, the curse, with which they died,
Had never passed away:
I could not draw my eyes from theirs,
Nor turn them up to pray.

And now this spell was snapt: once more
I viewed the ocean green,
And looked far forth, yet little saw
Of what had else been seen –

Like one, that on a lonesome road
Doth walk in fear and dread,
And having once turned round walks on,
And turns no more his head;
Because he knows, a frightful fiend
Doth close behind him tread.

But soon there breathed a wind on me,
Nor sound nor motion made:
Its path was not upon the sea,
In ripple or in shade.

It raised my hair, it fanned my cheek
Like a meadow-gale of spring –
It mingled strangely with my fears,
Yet it felt like a welcoming.

Swiftly, swiftly flew the ship,
Yet she sailed softly too;
Sweetly, sweetly blew the breeze –
On me alone it blew.

Oh! dream of joy! is this indeed
The light-house top I see?
Is this the hill? is this the kirk?
Is this mine own countree?

We drifted o'er the harbour-bar,
And I with sobs did pray –
O let me be awake, my God!
Or let me sleep alway.

The harbour-bay was clear as glass,
So smoothly it was strewn!
And on the bay the moonlight lay,
And the shadow of the Moon.

The rock shone bright, the kirk no less,
That stands above the rock:
The moonlight steeped in silentness
The steady weathercock.

And the bay was white with silent light,
Till rising from the same,

Full many shapes, that shadows were,
In crimson colours came.

A little distance from the prow
Those crimson shadows were:
I turned my eyes upon the deck –
Oh, Christ! what saw I there!

Each corse lay flat, lifeless and flat,
And, by the holy rood!
A man all light, a seraph-man,
On every corse there stood.

This seraph-band, each waved his hand:
It was a heavenly sight!
They stood as signals to the land,
Each one a lovely light;

This seraph-band, each waved his hand,
No voice did they impart –
No voice; but oh! the silence sank
Like music on my heart.

But soon I heard the dash of oars,
I heard the Pilot's cheer;
My head was turned perforce away,
And I saw a boat appear.

The Pilot and the Pilot's boy,
I heard them coming fast:
Dear Lord in Heaven! it was a joy
The dead men could not blast.

I saw a third – I heard his voice:
It is the Hermit good!
He singeth loud his godly hymns
That he makes in the wood.
He'll shrieve my soul, he'll wash away
The Albatross's blood.

PART VII

This hermit good lives in that wood
Which slopes down to the sea.
How loudly his sweet voice he rears!
He loves to talk with marineres
That come from a far countree.

He kneels at morn, and noon, and eve –
He hath a cushion plump:
It is the moss that wholly hides
The rotted old oak-stump.

The skiff-boat neared: I heard them talk,
'Why, this is strange, I trow!
Where are those lights so many and fair,
That signal made but now?'

'Strange, by my faith!' the Hermit said –
'And they answered not our cheer!
The planks looked warped! and see those sails,
How thin they are and sere!
I never saw aught like to them,
Unless perchance it were

Brown skeletons of leaves that lag
My forest-brook along;
When the ivy-tod is heavy with snow,
And the owlet whoops to the wolf below,
That eats the she-wolf's young.'

'Dear Lord! it hath a fiendish look –
(The Pilot made reply)
I am a-feared' – 'Push on, push on!'
Said the Hermit cheerily.

The boat came closer to the ship,
But I nor spake nor stirred;
The boat came close beneath the ship,
And straight a sound was heard.

Under the water it rumbled on,
Still louder and more dread:

It reached the ship, it split the bay;
The ship went down like lead.

Stunned by that loud and dreadful sound,
Which sky and ocean smote,
Like one that hath been seven days drowned
My body lay afloat;
But swift as dreams, myself I found
Within the Pilot's boat.

Upon the whirl, where sank the ship,
The boat spun round and round;
And all was still, save that the hill
Was telling of the sound.

I moved my lips – the Pilot shrieked
And fell down in a fit;
The holy Hermit raised his eyes,
And prayed where he did sit.

I took the oars: the Pilot's boy,
Who now doth crazy go,
Laughed loud and long, and all the while
His eyes went to and fro.
'Ha! ha!' quoth he, 'full plain I see,
The Devil knows how to row.'

And now, all in my own countree,
I stood on the firm land!
The Hermit stepped forth from the boat,
And scarcely he could stand.

'O shrieve me, shrieve me, holy man!'
The Hermit crossed his brow.
'Say quick,' quoth he, 'I bid thee say –
What manner of man art thou?'

Forthwith this frame of mine was wrenched
With a woful agony,
Which forced me to begin my tale;
And then it left me free.

Since then, at an uncertain hour,
That agony returns:

And till my ghastly tale is told,
This heart within me burns.

I pass, like night, from land to land;
I have strange power of speech;
That moment that his face I see,
I know the man that must hear me:
To him my tale I teach.

What loud uproar bursts from that door!
The wedding-guests are there:
But in the garden-bower the bride
And bride-maids singing are:
And hark the little vesper bell,
Which biddeth me to prayer!

O Wedding-Guest! this soul hath been
Alone on a wide wide sea:
So lonely 'twas, that God himself
Scarce seemed there to be.

O sweeter than the marriage-feast,
'Tis sweeter far to me,
To walk together to the kirk
With a goodly company! –

To walk together to the kirk,
And all together pray,
While each to his great Father bends,
Old men, and babes, and loving friends,
And youths and maidens gay!

Farewell, farewell! but this I tell
To thee, thou Wedding-Guest!
He prayeth well, who loveth well
Both man and bird and beast.

He prayeth best, who loveth best
All things both great and small;
For the dear God who loveth us,
He made and loveth all.

The Mariner, whose eye is bright,
Whose beard with age is hoar,
Is gone: and now the Wedding-Guest
Turned from the bridegroom's door.

He went like one that hath been stunned
And is of sense forlorn:
A sadder and a wiser man,
He rose the morrow morn.

SAMUEL TAYLOR COLERIDGE

PENGUIN POPULAR CLASSICS

Published or forthcoming

Louisa M. Alcott	Little Women
Jane Austen	Emma
	Mansfield Park
	Northanger Abbey
	Persuasion
	Pride and Prejudice
	Sense and Sensibility
Anne Brontë	Agnes Grey
	The Tenant of Wildfell Hall
Charlotte Brontë	Jane Eyre
	Shirley
	Villette
Emily Brontë	Wuthering Heights
John Buchan	The Thirty-Nine Steps
Lewis Carroll	Alice's Adventures in Wonderland
	Through the Looking Glass
John Cleland	Fanny Hill
Wilkie Collins	The Moonstone
	The Woman in White
Joseph Conrad	Heart of Darkness
	Lord Jim
	Nostromo
	The Secret Agent
	Victory
James Fenimore Cooper	The Last of the Mohicans
Stephen Crane	The Red Badge of Courage
Daniel Defoe	Moll Flanders
	Robinson Crusoe
Charles Dickens	Bleak House
	The Christmas Books Volume I
	David Copperfield
	Great Expectations
	Hard Times
	Little Dorrit
	Nicholas Nickleby
	Oliver Twist
	The Pickwick Papers
	A Tale of Two Cities

PENGUIN POPULAR CLASSICS

Published or forthcoming

Sir Arthur Conan Doyle	The Adventures of Sherlock Holmes
George Eliot	Adam Bede
	Middlemarch
	The Mill on the Floss
	Silas Marner
Henry Fielding	Tom Jones
F. Scott Fitzgerald	The Great Gatsby
Elizabeth Gaskell	Cranford
	Mary Barton
	North and South
Kenneth Grahame	The Wind in the Willows
H. Rider Haggard	King Solomon's Mines
	She
Thomas Hardy	Far from the Madding Crowd
	Jude the Obscure
	The Mayor of Casterbridge
	A Pair of Blue Eyes
	The Return of the Native
	Tess of the D'Urbervilles
	Under the Greenwood Tree
	The Woodlanders
Nathaniel Hawthorne	The Scarlet Letter
Henry James	The Ambassadors
	The Aspern Papers
	The Turn of the Screw
M. R. James	Ghost Stories
Rudyard Kipling	The Jungle Books
	Just So Stories
	Kim
	Plain Tales from the Hills
Jack London	White Fang/The Call of the Wild

PENGUIN POPULAR CLASSICS

Published or forthcoming

Herman Melville	Moby Dick
Francis Turner Palgrave	The Golden Treasury
Edgar Allan Poe	Selected Tales
Walter Scott	Ivanhoe
William Shakespeare	Antony and Cleopatra
	As You Like It
	Hamlet
	King Lear
	Macbeth
	The Merchant of Venice
	A Midsummer Night's Dream
	Othello
	Romeo and Juliet
	The Tempest
	Twelfth Night
Mary Shelley	Frankenstein
Robert Louis Stevenson	Dr Jekyll and Mr Hyde
	Kidnapped
	Treasure Island
Bram Stoker	Dracula
Jonathan Swift	Gulliver's Travels
W. M. Thackeray	Vanity Fair
Anthony Trollope	Barchester Towers
	Framley Parsonage
	The Warden
Mark Twain	Huckleberry Finn
	Tom Sawyer
Jules Verne	Around the World in Eighty Days
	Twenty Thousand Leagues Under the Sea
Oscar Wilde	Lord Arthur Saville's Crime
	The Picture of Dorian Gray